I, Q Series

Book One:
Independence Hall

Book Two:
The White House

Book Three:
Kitty Hawk

Book Four:
The Alamo

Book Five:
The Windy City

Book Six:
Alcatraz

I, Q

(Book Six: Alcatraz)

Roland Smith

and

Michael P. Spradlin

Sleeping Bear Press™

www.IQtheSeries.com

Copyright © 2014 Roland Smith
Copyright © 2014 Michael P. Spradlin

Library of Congress Cataloging-in-Publication Data

Smith, Roland, 1951-
Alcatraz / Roland Smith and Michael P. Spradlin.
pages cm.
Summary: "After thwarting the ghost cell's chemical attack in Chicago, Q and his stepsister Angela arrive in San Francisco to continue their parents' concert tour. They find themselves helping Boone and the S.O.S. team in the final showdown with the ghost cell and its leader, Number One"-- Provided by publisher.
ISBN 978-1-58536-826-6 (hard cover) -- ISBN 978-1-58536-825-9 (paperback)
[1. Spies--Fiction. 2. Terrorism--Fiction. 3. Stepfamilies--Fiction. 4. Musicians--Fiction. 5. San Francisco (Calif.)--Fiction. 6. Alcatraz Island (Calif.)--Fiction. 7. Mystery and detective stories.] I. Spradlin, Michael P. II. Title.
PZ7.S65766Alc 2014
[Fic]--dc23
2014016045

ISBN 978-1-58536-825-9
1 3 5 7 9 10 8 6 4 2

ISBN 978-1-58536-826-6 (case)
1 3 5 7 9 10 8 6 4 2

This book was typeset in Berthold Baskerville and Datum
Cover design by Lone Wolf Black Sheep
Cover illustration by Kaylee Cornfield

Printed in the United States.

Sleeping Bear Press™
315 E. Eisenhower Parkway, Suite 200
Ann Arbor, Michigan 48108

© 2014 Sleeping Bear Press
visit us at sleepingbearpress.com

For all my dedicated readers, but especially
Sophia Cajune.
−Roland

To Jessica Luca
For making our family complete
−Mike

Cast of Characters

Quest (Q) Munoz: Q is thirteen and wants to be a famous magician when he grows up. His idol is the great magician Harry Houdini. Q is ambivalent about school, but gets As in math and writing. He is seriously opposed to his new stepfather's vegetarianism and sneaks junk food at any opportunity. Tall with blond hair, he dresses the same way almost every day, usually in some variation of cargo pants or cargo shorts and a polo or T-shirt.

When Q is nervous, he shuffles cards and practices card tricks. It helps him relax and concentrate. He has a complicated relationship with his biological father, Speed Paulsen. Q is prone to premonitions, occasionally feeling that something bad is about to happen. He calls these feelings "the itch." The itch proves useful to Q and Angela on more than one occasion.

Angela Tucker: Angela, fifteen, has shoulder-length black hair with bangs, and olive skin. She has dark brown eyes and, upon first meeting her, Q thinks she is thin and a little frail-looking. But Angela is anything but frail. She wants to be a Secret Service agent like her mother, Malak Tucker, who died in the line of duty. Angela is smart, observant, and highly organized.

Angela always carries a small tattered backpack, in which she keeps extra hats, sunglasses, and other items that help her disguise her appearance when she practices her countersurveillance techniques and tradecraft (a term spies and agents use that refers to the techniques of trailing a suspect, eluding a tail, and other methods they use in performing their duties). Angela keeps her desire to be an agent secret from her father, Roger, who would not approve of her desire to join the Secret Service.

Blaze Munoz and Roger Tucker: Q's mom and Angela's dad have recently married. They are musicians and perform together as the duet Match. After marrying in a ceremony in San Francisco, they take Q and Angela on tour with them across the country.

Tyrone Boone: Boone is an old roadie (someone who travels with musicians and musical acts, performing all kinds of tasks on a tour). Boone is in charge of tour security and keeps an eye on Q and Angela. He travels with his very old, nearly toothless, and quite smelly dog, Croc. Boone is a former NOC (No Official Cover) agent for the CIA. He now uses a network of former spies to run "off-the-books" or unofficial operations.

Malak Tucker: Angela's mother and a United States Secret Service agent.

Eben Lavi: A rogue Mossad agent. (Mossad is roughly the Israeli equivalent of the CIA.) Eben is tracking a terrorist he believes is responsible for his brother's death. He believes the assassin known as "the Leopard" has a connection to Angela.

Ziv: The mysterious Ziv is a NOC agent for Mossad.

Buddy T.: Buddy T. is Blaze and Roger's manager. Though he is obnoxious and offensive in practically every way, he's still one of the most successful managers in the music business. Roger jokes that the "T" stands for "To-Do," because when Buddy talks he sounds like he's giving everyone a "to-do" list.

J. R. Culpepper: J.R. is the president of the United States, or POTUS, as he is referred to by the Secret Service. Before being elected president he served in the U.S. Senate, was vice president, and was director of the CIA.

Marie and Art: Marie and Art are Roger's and Blaze's personal assistants, or PAs. Buddy T. thinks that he hired them but in fact they are highly trained agents and bodyguards working for Boone.

Heather Hughes: Heather is the president of a record company and responsible in large part for putting Match back on the charts. She knows Boone well from all her years in the music industry. Mostly her job appears to be keeping Buddy T. mollified and out of everyone's way.

P.K.: P.K. is short for President's Kid, the Secret Service code name for Willingham Culpepper, son of J. R. Culpepper. P.K. is ten years old, but smarter than most and wise beyond his years. He knows the location of many of the secret passages in the White House and has a Secret Service radio, which he uses to keep tabs on the agents so that he can practice eluding them.

Bethany Culpepper: J.R. is widowed and his daughter, Bethany, takes on the role of first lady.

Speed Paulsen: Q's biological father. Speed is a rock star and loves to play the part. He earned the nickname Speed because he could pick guitar strings faster than anyone alive. It's been a while since Speed has had any hit songs and he is jealous of his ex-wife's sudden, newfound success. Speed is annoying, hapless, confused, in and out of rehab, but at the same time strangely likeable.

Agent Pat Callaghan: A Secret Service agent assigned to Boone's team. Callaghan is capable, trustworthy, and devoted to J.R. and his family.

The SOS team: A group of Boone's most trusted operatives. SOS stands for "Some Old Spooks." The team consists of:

X-Ray: The technical genius. He spends most of his time in a van the team calls the "intellimobile." There is no computer system and no database or piece of electronic equipment X-Ray cannot hack, master, construct, or duplicate.

Vanessa: The team's designated "world's deadliest old broad." She is a master knife thrower, and Boone refers to her as a "human lie detector" due to her ability to read people and determine if they are telling the truth. Vanessa is also an exceptional driver and adept at tailing suspects without being noticed.

Felix and Uly: Formal Special Forces operatives. Given their size (both are nearly six feet eight inches tall) and matching buzz cuts, they could easily be mistaken for brothers. Their strength, expertise in hand-to-hand combat, and knowledge of nearly every type of weapon imaginable make them invaluable members of Boone's squad.

MONDAY, SEPTEMBER 15 >

8:00 a.m. to 11:00 a.m. PST

The Ghost

The apartment's balcony stood empty. Without warning, Number One appeared there, silently and with only the barest movement of the surrounding air. It was as if he had stepped through some invisible curtain onto a stage: not there; then, unexpectedly, there. His face was drenched in sweat and his knees buckled. Unable to keep his feet, he collapsed, clutching at the balcony railing for support. He leaned forward, his head resting against the cool metal. Exhaustion racked his body. In the past ten days he had used his ability at unprecedented levels. It was taking a fearsome toll on him.

Ever since he had first gained his power hundreds of years ago, the things he could do never ceased to amaze him. Yet all power came with consequences. Now the cost of his gift racked him with pain and nausea. He slowed his breathing and closed his eyes. There was much to do, and use of his power would be required again soon. After a few minutes he gathered himself and stood up straight, groaning with the effort. He stood still, letting the cool breeze blow over him.

The balcony overlooked the city below and it was a grand view. Farther out, the blue water of the bay sparkled brightly in the sunlight. Despite all the things he had seen in his life—and he had been to every corner of the world—he still marveled at the Golden Gate Bridge. There was something about this massive feat of human ingenuity juxtaposed against the natural beauty of the bay that stirred him. A small part of him was saddened that it would all have to be destroyed.

Now that he knew everything he needed to know, he would bring it all crashing down. Western Civilization, as it currently existed, would end. For hundreds of years he had waited—no, he had yearned—for this moment. And although he was physically drained and desperately needed time to rest and recharge, he was also excited.

This apartment was one of the few places in the world he could truly relax and be himself. He had others like it in several other cities: Los Angeles; New York; London; Brussels; and Istanbul. But this haven in San Francisco was his favorite. It was the ideal place for him to recover from what had been a very busy few days.

Stepping inside the apartment he glanced at his reflection in a large mirror that hung on the wall. He looked tired and weak. He aged slowly, but he had aged nevertheless. When he first gained the ability he was so young. In the hundreds of years he had been alive, he had changed his name, identity, and look so many times that there were days he scarcely recognized the man who stared back at him from inside the glass.

To the hundreds of members of his organization he was

Number One, leader of the ghost cell. And his current public persona was perfect for running the organization. It allowed him to travel to a variety of cities and countries. It kept him near people who had great amounts of money and influence. But he had been alive for so long that sometimes it felt like he couldn't remember his real name. And he often speculated whether a "real" name mattered to someone who had lived through dozens of lifetimes.

For many years he had wondered (and occasionally worried) that his grand plan—to destroy the West and restore the Caliphate—might not be possible. Western technology and military superiority had advanced. His people had spent centuries fighting amongst themselves. But in the last fifty years, as their numbers grew, the tide had turned. Westerners had become lazy and distracted.

Now he was poised to bring it all crashing down. Once he had the item back in his possession, he would begin. He would use its power to raise even more warriors just like himself, all with the same unique capability. With their newfound power he would place loyalists in positions of power around the globe. He would raise an army that would wrest control of the very bedrock of the West. Such an army would be unstoppable.

But like everything else, wars must happen at the proper time. He had things to do first. The most important was to make sure that that moron Buddy T. found the item. Buddy had the badly mistaken notion that he was going to escape. No. Buddy could never escape him. No one could. But he would recover the item first and then he would deal with his idiotic underling.

For a moment he cursed himself for giving it to Buddy in the first place, though he could not have risked having it discovered. The best security systems in the world could be beaten. He should know—he'd defeated most of them himself. That was why he'd entrusted it to Buddy T. The man had no idea what it was. To him it was just another piece of art or some other valuable antique locked in a weird-looking container. Another trinket among the hundreds of others he had given him over the years. And Buddy was far too terrified of him to do anything stupid.

Traveling from town to town, on the road all the time, it made more sense to keep it safely locked away. The power it possessed was the key to everything. When he first realized he would live far longer than a normal human being, he'd always kept it nearby. For centuries he had studied the box that somehow kept the item concealed from him. He tried hundreds of different ways to open it, to unlock its secrets. And up to this point, opening the box was the only thing in his life he had ever failed at. Finally, a few years ago, he'd decided to have Buddy hide it. He would instead devote his efforts to finding the one he knew would be able to open it and give him what he wanted.

That was a perilous path in its own right.

In recent years, Western intelligence agencies had grown smarter, more cunning and capable. Despite his carefully crafted secret, he was not so foolish as to believe he could not be identified or even captured one day. At times like this, when he could not use his ability, he was as weak and vulnerable as any mortal man. Keeping the item locked away, where he had no knowledge of its whereabouts, was insurance. If he were to be captured and put in a place he could not escape from (and there were such places) he would not be able to reveal its location.

He entered the apartment from the balcony door. How he loved this place. It had been built with the millions of dollars he had accumulated over the centuries. The rest of the building was empty. Bribes and payoffs kept the code inspectors and other city officials away. No one had ever visited here. Had he allowed someone in, they would find the top floor of the building to be a virtual museum of music history.

The walls were covered in photographs. Many of them showed him posing next to famous musicians, rock stars, and other celebrities. There were framed concert posters, programs, and playbills for performances that dated back to the eighteenth century. There were musical instruments in display cases. One of them held a Stradivarius violin. Inside another was one of the first Fender electric guitars. There were even pictures of him with presidents and heads of state from all over the world.

A long, luxurious leather couch occupied the center of the living room. He plopped his tired body down on it and kicked off his cowboy boots. Leaning back, he laid his head on the headrest, closing his eyes. In his mind, he recounted everywhere he'd been in the last few days: Philadelphia; Washington, D.C.; Kitty Hawk; San Antonio; and Chicago. Not to mention all the small towns and cities in between as he'd crisscrossed the country. It had been exhausting but necessary, and his current public persona was one of his greatest creations. Living as long as he had, moving in and out and around the people in the music business, he'd managed to fool them all.

Then there was the ghost cell. His brilliance had built an organization that had endured for centuries. For hundreds of generations it had struck fear into the hearts of the infidels. And while his enemies grew smarter and used technology and better intelligence to their advantage, so did he. He had not idly watched as times changed. He used the same, if not better, resources that they did.

And at last, after hundreds of years of searching, he finally found the one other person in the world who shared his ability. He remembered the night he first found him—on a battlefield, gravely wounded and clutching the box in his hands. Whatever was inside it gave off a strange and mysterious glow. Number One had finally understood that whatever it was, it was the object inside the mysterious box that gave both of them the ability. He was sure of it. But the man had sealed it up before he could grab it.

It had taken centuries but at last he had found him.

Now he would not let Buddy escape before he brought him the box. He would capture this man and convince him to reveal the secrets of the source of their power. It had taken so long. The identity of the man had truly surprised him. The fact that they had crossed paths professionally so many times before was ironic and truly mind-boggling.

He let his mind drift. He was so tired. All he needed to do now was rest. After the man told him what he needed to know, Number One would kill him. Then no one could stop him.

Kill him.

He wondered about death. Just because they could use the incredible power they'd been given, he knew they could still be killed. Or could they? Yes, they aged slowly and the power they had to move about so quickly also slowed the aging process, but was it really immortality? What would he do if the other man could not be killed and managed to stop him? Or he would not reveal the secret of their ability? Maybe they *were* immortal. They both had grown older. Perhaps the two of them had simply been granted an extended life. Whatever power the item granted them merely slowed their aging process. Since they had both aged, maybe they would both die one day.

But not yet.

Not before he learned what he needed to know.

It was time to complete his mission. He ran through the details again in his mind.

All he had to do was wait for Buddy's call. Everything was in place. All the players were here in San Francisco. He could rest.

Number One smiled, closing his eyes and running his fingers through his long hair.

If he wasn't so tired, he would have stood up and danced.

Reality Bites

"They can send me to boarding school, but they'll never take my freedom," I said.

Angela chuckled.

"Why are you laughing?" I asked her. "This is serious. You realize after the concert tonight we're going to be put in . . . I can't say it."

"I'm laughing because even when you're freaking out you can still be funny. And you need to lighten up. Boarding school isn't the worst thing in the world," Angela said.

Easy for her to say. Whoever invented a school you had to live at was obviously evil. I'll bet the ghost cell invented boarding schools. It was the most malicious thing I could think of. I couldn't quite grasp how she could be so nonchalant about it.

On the other hand, it was nice to see that Angela had finally relaxed a little. We were sitting in the back of Agent Callaghan's rental car. We had picked it up at the airport and were circling around to where the cargo terminals were located. Boone and the SOS crew had arrived there right as we'd landed. I'd had a little dustup with my mom over a Kit Kat bar. Actually I was just trying to create a diversion because this ginormous plane carrying the Match tour's coach was visible out the window of the terminal. I didn't want Mom or Roger to see it. So I'd bought a Kit Kat from the gift shop and scarfed it down right in front of them. Mom got mad (but not so mad that she didn't filch a piece of chocolate before she made me throw it out) and Roger had looked perplexed. Roger is a vegetarian. I wanted to point out that a Kit Kat bar is technically vegetarian, but thought better of it. He's against junk food too.

Anyway, I was in big trouble and Agent Callaghan had deftly interceded on my behalf. He told Mom and Roger that until Boone caught up with us, he (Callaghan) was still technically in charge of our security. So he'd take us to our hotel, get us checked in, and make sure we were safe. After everything that had happened the last few days–there had been terrorist attacks in L.A. and Atlanta–I think Mom and Roger were secretly happy to have a U.S. Secret Service agent watching over us. Mom had promised me that we'd "discuss my rude behavior" later, right before Agent Callaghan spirited us away.

"Don't be so dramatic," Angela said, bringing me back from my reflection on how much trouble I was in.

"I thought you said I was being funny."

Angela rolled her eyes and chuckled. Before we left Chicago, she received a text from Ziv–she'd recently learned he was her grandfather–that her mom was safe. *Safe for now,*

I thought to myself. Ever since we met Boone and all of this started, I'd learned that "safe" was a very fluid term.

Agent Callaghan was using a Bluetooth headset as he drove. I didn't know who he was talking to, but he was using words like "sit-rep," which meant situation report. I knew this because I'd been hanging around a bunch of spies.

"Dramatic? *I'm* being dramatic? Do you want me to run through everything we've been through in the last few days? Starting with the pigeon poop in Philadelphia?" I asked.

"No, I'm good," Angela said.

"As a matter of fact, you are in a happy place," I said. I just wanted to point it out to her before she got gloomy again. Angela could be a little moody.

"Right—because I know my mom is okay," she said. "At least for now."

One thing about having Angela as a stepsister was that it had made me do a lot of thinking in the past few days. The entire flight out here, I was a jumble of all kinds of emotions. There were a lot of reasons why, not all of them having to do with having to go to boarding school. A lot of bad stuff happened while we were on tour. I'd seen things I could never unsee. Angela and I were helping Boone and his group of former spies track down these bad guys, which had put us in some very hairy situations.

Except that now there had been horrible terrorist attacks in L.A. and Atlanta. We'd stopped them from executing their plan in Chicago, which would have made the total casualties a much higher number. Then there was the fact that, in Chicago, we discovered we had a ghost cell member right in the middle of our tour.

Buddy T.

He was Mom and Roger's manager. He'd walked off the job in a huff right before their last concert. Only it was all an act. Buddy was involved in everything right up to his perpetually red face.

There was another reason why remaining on the tour was vital. Not just because I wanted to see the ghost cell destroyed and brought to justice. I also had a personal reason.

When Angela and I were on the rooftop of the Hancock building in Chicago, a terrorist had been just about to shoot her. I saw the red laser-targeting dot on her forehead. She was going to die within seconds. Before I even realized what happened, I *poofed!* just like Boone. I zoomed across the rooftop and knocked her out of the way. The bullets missed her by inches. But it scared me. And I was still scared. What if I did it again? I didn't even know what it was I was doing! Which was why I needed to talk to Boone. He did it all the time. He was a *poof!* expert. A poofpert.

And if I got shipped off to Screwupmylife Boarding Academy, well, it would be a lot harder to get answers out of Boone. Because he wouldn't be there, being that he was so busy chasing terrorists. I had to figure out a way to get back in Mom's good graces and get her to change her mind. I pulled out my phone and texted her that I was sorry about my behavior at the airport. I asked her to forgive me. I hoped it helped.

If I was being honest, I didn't blame Mom or Roger for the boarding school thing. I'd probably do the same if I were in their place. It just couldn't happen in the next couple of days. I needed to talk to Boone. And so did Angela, for that matter.

And so Agent Callaghan took pity on me. Probably figured chasing terrorists was safer than being around my mom when she was really angry—and he wasn't completely wrong. Now we were on our way to meet up with the SOS crew again.

Everyone on the plane had been quiet and somber on the flight out. The terrorist attacks had cast a pall over the entire country, and our little group was no different. It was all anyone could really talk about, and it was always on the news. The thing was, very few people knew all the things Angela and I knew. Like, the ghost cell. That Angela's mother was still alive. That we'd helped save the president's daughter from terrorist kidnappers. And all the other stuff. It was a walk on a delicate tightrope to keep our parents from finding out. And actually, Buddy T. disappearing worked to our immediate advantage, in a way.

Things were chaotic with the tour because Buddy T. threw a huge fit in Chicago and quit. As the tour manager he took care of a lot of details. His leaving forced Mom, Roger, and Heather to scramble while they dealt with many of the duties Buddy usually handled. Heather Hughes was the president of Mom and Roger's record company and she'd stepped in as temporary tour manager when Buddy disappeared.

Only Buddy T. hadn't really walked off the job after his little performance in Chicago. He was part of the ghost cell. Buddy helped put the chemical weapon on top of the John Hancock Center building in Chicago. He was deeply involved in all the bad stuff that had happened in the last few weeks. And now he was on the run.

We knew Boone had to come to San Francisco to maintain his cover on the tour. But we hadn't heard from him until he'd called and said we should meet at the airport. It made sense, given that this whole thing had started when we left San Francisco right after Mom and Roger got married. Buddy lived in San Francisco; he was probably coming back to get his money and whatever else he needed to disappear.

At least that was our guess. We'd been hanging out at the hotel in Chicago, because after the attacks all the flights were grounded. If I had to guess, I'd bet Boone called POTUS–the president of the United States, J. R. Culpepper, who we'd had the pleasure of meeting and who'd given us really cool spy watches at the White House. The president had arranged for them to use a big military cargo plane to get everything out here once the flight restrictions were lifted.

But right now we had no clue what Boone and his team were planning or what they'd managed to find out about Buddy. Once we got to the terminal I guessed we'd get briefed and he'd give us something to do.

Otherwise, we were going to be stuck in another hotel room for a while, at least until the boarding school enrollment happened. It made me really hope Boone would have a job for us. Hotels now officially gave me the heebie-jeebies. I'd been kidnapped from one in San Antonio. A terrorist had been staying right down the hall for the last week. I was beginning to think I should take up camping. Being in a tent surrounded by grizzly bears couldn't be any more dangerous than our lives had become since we met Tyrone Boone.

Agent Callaghan disconnected his call. "I've got something to tell you. Two things, actually," he said. Agent Callaghan looks like he just stepped off a recruiting poster for the Secret Service. He has this strong, square jaw. His eyes are kind of a steel-gray color. But the one thing you notice about him most is his . . . I guess you'd call it presence. When you first glance at him, he's tall and kind of a good-looking guy. But when you look deeper, you see he has this attitude about him. You instantly get a feeling that while he might be friendly, he's not someone you want to mess with. If you did, he'd make you regret it. Probably fifty different ways. With his pinkie.

"First, I just have to tell you how much the two of you have impressed me the past few days. Boone briefed me about your involvement in the Chicago op. And this whole thing with your parents sending you to boarding school? Most kids would cave, start whining, and tell their parents everything they knew if they thought it would get them out of it. But not you two. Angela, it's unreal how much you remind me of your mother. And Q, you sure do some quick thinking. That little performance with the Kit Kat bar was smart. I just wanted you to know you've both done a good job in a very difficult situation."

Angela blushed and I shrugged. But it was kind of a cool thing for him to say. When you get praise from a guy trained to take a bullet for someone else, it tends to mean a little more than the average compliment.

"The other thing is, that was Boone on the phone. X-Ray has some leads on Buddy T. We need bodies to run surveillance. When we get to the hangar we'll figure out where we need to set up."

"Is my mom there?" Angela asked.

"Ziv texted Boone. They're going to be there any minute," he said. "They've been driving out from Chicago. You know Ziv, he wouldn't trust any kind of public transportation."

Angela sat back in her seat and smiled. I was secretly glad that Malak and Ziv were on the way. The more people we had who could beat up terrorists the better, as far as I was concerned.

The car slowed and Agent Callaghan turned it onto an access road leading to the cargo terminal. Up ahead I could see the coach, the Range Rover, and the intellimobile. It looked like they were all here.

It was time to catch up with everyone.

The Monkey and the Leopard

The gray Buick sedan exited the freeway, heading toward the San Francisco airport. Ziv was at the wheel. Malak, who had been restlessly sleeping in the passenger seat, sat up.

"We're here?" she mumbled, still groggy from her nap.

Ziv, as he often did, said nothing.

Malak rubbed her eyes. It had been a long trip. Spending this much time in a car with Ziv had been revealing. She had a much better understanding of why she had always felt so safe when he was watching her in her guise as the Leopard.

Ziv was quite possibly the most paranoid person she had ever met.

Had they taken turns driving, they could have likely reached San Francisco in two days once they left Chicago. But Ziv would not hear of it. He drove. In four days on the road, they had changed vehicles six times. All of them rented under different identities Ziv carried with him.

They took circuitous routes and back roads. Ziv had particular requirements of the small motels they stayed in. No nice places or chains. "Too many records and cameras," he'd said. They stayed at small, privately owned places in out-of-the-way, off-the-grid locations. Always, they paid in cash.

Whenever they traveled a freeway, Ziv would exit every fifty miles or so, then turn around and drive back the same direction they had just come from.

"What are you doing?" Malak asked the first time he'd done it.

"Watching," he said. As if that was all the explanation that was required.

No wonder the Leopard had never been caught.

Malak stretched and rolled her shoulders, trying to get the muscles in her neck to relax. She reached into the waistband of her blue jeans and removed her automatic pistol. Racking the slide, she chambered a round, making sure the safety was on.

"No, daughter," Ziv said quietly. At first, Malak almost didn't realize he was speaking. Because he would remain silent for hours at a time, the sound of his voice often startled her.

"What?" she asked.

"No. Put the gun away," he said.

His eyes never left the road, and he maneuvered the car deftly through the airport traffic.

"No? What no? I'm just—"

"Put it away," he said. "There is no need."

"Need? Need for what? I—"

Ziv held up one hand to interrupt her. He sighed. She realized he must be tired but he would never admit it.

"Do you think I do not know what you plan to do? The

Monkey who watches the Leopard's tail? I know what you are thinking. Many times I know it before you do."

"What am I thinking, Ziv?"

"You are thinking, and have been since we left Grant Park in Chicago, about the identity of Number One and who it was that set you up to die."

"So?"

"So when we are nearly ready to rendezvous with Boone and his team you check your weapon? All these days on the road, you have been running down a list of suspects in your mind. Your plan now is to confront Boone. To force him to admit that either he is Number One or he knows who is. You will do it at gunpoint if required."

"That . . . no . . . I just–"

"Enough. Boone is not the enemy."

Malak looked out the window. It was uncanny how Ziv had been able to read her mind. She *was* planning to confront Boone. There were too many mysteries surrounding him. In truth, from the time J. R. Culpepper had been vice president and she served on his security detail, Malak had never trusted Boone completely. He and J.R. were friendly. Even back then she had heard rumors that Boone was NOC–No Official Cover–and that he and J.R. had worked together for years. Back when J.R. ran the Central Intelligence Agency.

But to her, there had always been something a little off about Boone. He made her suspicious. At Kitty Hawk she had demanded he make sure Angela and Q were kept safe and he'd delivered. But since then there had been so many strange things.

In Texas, Miss Ruby—Number Three in the ghost cell—had put her in a guesthouse next to the landing strip on her ranch. She was to await her plane to Chicago there. She had been frantic at being ordered away from Angela. But she couldn't break her cover. When she came out of the guesthouse bathroom, there sat Boone and his weird old dog, Croc, in the small living room. They had crossed several hundred yards of wide-open space, passed by Miss Ruby's constantly patrolling security teams (not to mention her electronic surveillance), and waltzed into the place like it was no big deal.

He claimed his tech man, X-Ray, had given him a device to distort electronic surveillance. All right. Maybe he had. But the guesthouse was in the middle of a wide-open ranch. How could a man and a dog, especially a man Boone's age, have crossed that distance unseen? At the time, not thinking clearly, she'd let it go.

But the events in the safe house in Chicago had ratcheted up her distrust. Someone had gotten into the house several times, eluding even the ever-watchful eyes of Ziv. They came in and left a package with a cell phone. And for a time she was certain they were there in the house when she was. Right in the next room. But as she cleared the house, room by room, no one was ever there. Then she would hear the back door click shut. She was certain someone was toying with her.

Once, before leaving the house, she sprinkled a fine coating of baby powder on the floor right in front of the door. When she returned she found footprints. She had not been crazy. Someone had visited while she was out. The footprints had been made by cowboy boots. Boone wore cowboy boots.

He was the only one who knew where she was besides Ziv, Eben, and Callaghan. It had to be him.

Then Buddy had stormed off and turned out to be involved in the plot. She found it all too convenient. Boone had known Buddy for years. They appeared to dislike each other a great deal. But what if it was all an act?

So many things about Boone didn't add up. And she intended to get answers.

"You don't understand," she said.

"Understand what? You have questions about Boone? Fine. Ask your questions. But not at the point of a gun."

"He . . . there's something . . ."

"Daughter," Ziv sighed. "You are tired. You are also brave and fearless. No one should or could have to sacrifice as much as you have for the duty you have undertaken. But you have been undercover a long time. Perhaps too long. I have seen it happen to many before you. You are the Leopard but you are not invulnerable. Your paranoia and suspicion have kept you alive. But in the last few days, so has Tyrone Boone."

"I just want answers," she said.

"As do I. I agree with you, Boone is mysterious. But he has kept his word. Angela is alive and safe. All of us are alive and safe. And we are close to ending this. You cannot go charging in demanding answers. Wait. Be patient. I do not claim to understand everything that is going on here. But I do know this. Boone is not the one you seek."

"How do you know?"

"The Monkey knows."

Malak could not help it—it made her chuckle. She returned

the pistol to its holster.

"All right, Ziv," she said. "We'll play it your way. Boone gets a pass."

Ziv nodded.

"For now," Malak said.

Reunion

Boone and Croc strolled into the hangar to find the SOS crew readying the vehicles for surveillance. The team didn't know it, but he and Croc had been in San Francisco for four days. Right after everything that happened in Chicago. They didn't need to wait for J.R. to lift the flight restrictions. Of course he couldn't let the team know that. Once here, he'd begun looking everywhere he could for any lead on Buddy or where he might be or where he might be headed. He and Croc had been watching train and bus stations, car rental agencies, staking out the house Buddy lived in before they'd left on tour. But there had been no sign of him.

By now, "blinking" had taken a lot out of him. The last day he'd taken time to rest, but he was still not back up to speed. He was glad to have his team here with him.

The back door of the intellimobile was open and X-Ray was tapping away at a keyboard. Vanessa had her wooden board set up in a corner and was tossing knives at it. Uly was loading a cooler of bottled water into the Range Rover and

Felix was doing a weapons check. Eben was pacing.

"Boone!" Eben said. "You're here? Where have you been? You weren't on our flight. How did you arrive in San Francisco so quickly? The commercial flights just started up again—"

"POTUS put us on a fighter jet," Boone interrupted.

"A fighter—excuse me?" Eben said, confused. "With your dog?"

"Yes. Croc wasn't crazy about the helmet," Boone said.

"You must . . . are . . . is he joking?" Eben asked Felix and Uly, both of whom only shrugged.

"Croc is what you'd call a nervous flyer; his stomach gets a little upset."

Everyone had gathered around Boone and Croc when they arrived. Now they instinctively took a step back. Croc stretched out on the hangar floor. His stomach made a rumbling sound. Everyone took another step back.

"X-Ray, what have you got?" Boone said, getting right to business. X-Ray stopped typing and swiveled around to face the open back of the van. A printer whirred and spat out several sheets of paper.

"Buddy T. is careful. And tricky. And smart. And careful," X-Ray said.

"You already said careful," Uly pointed out.

"Yeah. Well. You have no idea how long this took. Nothing is registered under his name, except at Bank of America where he has checking, savings, and IRA accounts like a normal citizen. Buddy has done well for himself money-wise. But I figured if he's at or near the top of the cell, he's got to have access to some of its money. What they do—the resources they have—it requires huge amounts of cash."

X-Ray handed out the sheets of paper, so everyone had a copy.

"Buddy was—or is—based in San Francisco. I started with local banks. Long story short, I started looking for money going from banks here to the obvious offshore places. Switzerland, the Cayman Islands. Finally found it in the Cook Islands," he said.

"Where the heck is that?" Felix asked.

"Near New Zealand," Boone said. "Has some of the most stringent banking privacy laws in the world and people seldom think to look there because it's so hard to reach. You can hop a flight to the Caymans from the States with a briefcase full of cash and stash it in a bank within a few hours. But it takes a lot of time and effort to get to the Cook Islands, so law enforcement seldom thinks to look there. If you're a crook or a terrorist, you've obviously got to be careful moving money online. There's always a chance you'll slip up. Then somebody like X-Ray finds you. Given how careful the ghost cell is, the Cook Islands makes perfect sense."

"Anyway," X-Ray continued. "I looked for money moving back and forth and found more than a dozen banks in the area sending and receiving wire transfers to and from banks in the Cook Islands. When I locked onto the account numbers, I was able to get into the banks' records on this end. It's a lot easier to get banks to open their records when they believe you work for the Department of Homeland Security," he said proudly.

"So, once I discovered the particular set of accounts, I checked the names on the accounts, and guess who the account holder was in every case?" X-Ray asked.

"I'll bet it starts with Buddy and ends with T." Vanessa said.

"Yep. Under fake names of course, but you always have to show photo ID. Buddy tried to change his appearance in a couple of cases. You can dye your hair, wear glasses and a fake mustache, but you can't fool photo recognition software these days. And there's something else," he said.

"Safe-deposit boxes," Boone said quietly.

"How did you guess?" X-Ray said, impressed.

"It only makes sense. He'd want some liquid assets handy. Cash, maybe uncut diamonds, bearer bonds. Stuff you could take with you easily if you had to run. We know Buddy T. is in this up to his ears. Now he's headed for his stash. Or stashes," Boone said.

"Well, the good news is, as far as I can tell he hasn't shown up anywhere to do or take anything yet," X-Ray said.

"What about the van they found outside Chicago–any word on identification of the body?" Felix asked.

The van Buddy and his terrorist pals had used to deliver the chemical weapon to the John Hancock Center was discovered in a deserted lot near O'Hare International Airport. It had been set on fire, and the FBI had recovered a single body, burned beyond recognition but still wearing recognizable yellow high-top tennis shoes and a melted Rolex watch on its wrist. Buddy had last been seen wearing those same shoes and watch.

"No ID yet, but it's not going to be Buddy. It was one of his stooges. I'm betting he shot him, then torched the van," Boone said. "He'll show up here soon. And when he does, we'll be waiting."

X-Ray rubbed his hands through his white hair. He had a three-day growth of beard, and it looked like it had been at least that long since he'd slept. "That's the thing, there's more banks than we have people. Even if we have only one person watching each bank, we're still going to be short. I can watch the security feeds from the banks' cameras for some of them and call out if he shows up. But if he goes someplace where we don't have someone on site, he could be gone before we can get there," X-Ray explained.

"Then it is a good thing we are here to help," a voice said from the doorway.

The team looked around to see Ziv and Malak strolling through the hangar door.

"I was wondering when you guys would show up," Boone said.

"I'm sure you were," Malak said. Boone gave her a curious look. She held his gaze until he looked away.

"As soon as Callaghan gets here with Q and Angela, we'll get to work."

Croc curled up on the floor of the hangar at Boone's feet and went to sleep.

Tension

We must have arrived just seconds after Malak and Ziv. I heard Malak say something, then Angela screamed, "Mom!" and ran to her, drowning out her words. Malak turned around just in time to catch Angela, and they almost tumbled to the ground, they were hugging each other so tightly. I have to say it did lift my mood a little.

Everyone was quiet while Angela and Malak held each other. Out of the corner of my eye, I'm pretty sure I saw Felix wipe away a tear. Malak broke the embrace, taking Angela's hands in her own. She looked her up and down and smiled and hugged her again.

"Mom, are you okay?" Angela asked.

"I'm fine, sweetheart. I'm fine," Malak said.

"How did you get through security to the terminal?" Callaghan asked.

"Did you not know, Agent Callaghan, that I am a member of your Homeland Security Agency?" Ziv replied.

Callaghan chuckled. "No, I didn't know that."

Everyone let Malak and Angela enjoy the reunion for a short while longer before Boone got back to business.

"I believe you were saying something about surveillance?" Ziv asked.

"Um. Yes," Boone said. "Here is the list of banks again; I've divided them up. I know we're short on people, but I don't want to send anyone out alone. X has divided the city up into zones based on the location of each bank. Each team will go to the most central location in each zone for onsite surveillance. X-Ray will cover the rest by hacking their security camera feeds. If Buddy hits a bank where we don't have someone, he'll send the closest team and the rest of us will come running. I've asked J.R. and he's promised us more bodies as soon as he can spare them. But with the attacks . . . for now it's just us."

Croc was now sitting on his haunches; his stomach rumbled and growled. A few seconds later, the rankest odor I'd ever smelled in my life wafted through the air. In another few seconds, everyone was scurrying for a vehicle.

"Me and Uly got the Rover," Felix yelled.

"I'll take X-Ray in the intellimobile," Vanessa said. X-Ray rolled his chair backward into the van and slammed the rear doors. Vanessa hustled into the driver's seat. We heard the doors lock as the engine roared to life.

Felix and Uly peeled out of the hangar in the Range Rover, followed closely by the intellimobile.

"Huh," Boone said. "I guess the rest of us will have to take the coach."

"Not me," Callaghan said. "Rented a car. I need to have

Angela and Q with me in case their parents call. Come on, guys," he said, waving his hand in front of his face, trying to disperse the odor that was now rolling through the hangar like fog.

"Okay, then," Boone said. "That leaves the rest of us in the coach. Ziv, Malak, I'd like you to come with us. We can fill you in on what we know. We'll split up into our two-man teams after you've been briefed."

Ziv looked down at Croc. "If we must," he said.

"Great," Boone said. "Let's get to it."

He and Croc climbed aboard the coach with Ziv, Malak, and Eben following along reluctantly. Malak stopped to give Angela a hug. I'm not sure what they said. Being apart from her mom was killing her. But Angela knew she and I had to stay with Callaghan for the time being, at least.

"Wonderful," Eben complained as he climbed aboard. He muttered something in Hebrew. I had no idea what it was, but it wouldn't have surprised me if it was "Blast Boone and his stinky dog."

Sometimes Surveillance Is Just Showing Up

We had been assigned a bank in the Mission District of San Francisco. Agent Callaghan seemed to know the city pretty well. I would imagine Secret Service agents had to have a pretty good knowledge of most major cities. Presidents tended to travel a lot.

On our way, Callaghan stopped at a convenience store to buy stakeout supplies. But not before giving us a "don't mess with me, I'm a Secret Service agent and if you try sneaking away or anything remotely funny I will find you" speech. While we waited in the backseat I fidgeted, and Angela stared at her phone. Like totally absorbed stared.

"What are you looking at?" I asked.

"This last photo of the statue that P.K. sent us. We know it's Boone and P.K. said it was on the estate of an Italian nobleman."

"Yeah? So?"

"I think it's more than that. Look at the statue. He's wearing chain mail and holding a sword. I think he was a knight."

"You mean like a King Arthur Round Table–type knight?"

"No, Q, King Arthur was probably historically real, but the Round Table part is most likely fiction. I mean a real knight. Most of the nobility in the Middle Ages had one or more of their sons knighted."

"How do you know all this stuff?" I was genuinely curious.

"It's called books, Q. Remember when we first met Boone and he said everything you need to know can be found in books?"

"Sort of. Meeting Boone seems like it happened years ago."

"Well, Boone was right. Wouldn't kill you to read a book once in a while."

"I read. Ask me anything about Harry Houdini. And I just started *From Russia, With Love* by Ian Fleming."

"Yeah. Whatever. Still. Say Boone was a knight. P.K. says he hasn't found anything on Boone beyond the date of this statue. And with the crumbling foundation, some of the letters are missing. It's like a word jumble, except in Latin."

"Huh. Boone was a knight. Maybe that explains why he's been in so many wars and stuff."

"Maybe. But if we can figure out what it says . . . we might get closer to figuring out who Boone is."

"Put P.K. on it," I said. "Kid loves a puzzle. He's probably got access to some big supercomputer or something."

P.K. was short for President's Kid. We had met him in the White House at the beginning of the tour. He was quite possibly the smartest ten-year-old I'd ever met. Malak had managed to keep P.K. and us from getting kidnapped by a couple of deep-cover ghost cell agents who had infiltrated the White House.

"Way ahead of you. He is working on it. But P.K. can't do everything. He has school. The Secret Service is watching him. He'll let us know if he finds anything."

"You sure there was no actual round table for King Arthur's knights to sit around?" I said.

"Yes, Q. It's called a myth. Each knight of the Round Table represented a virtue like courage, honesty—"

I interrupted her. "Yeah, I saw the movie. But what I mean is, didn't knights belong to groups? Like the Knights of the Round Table? The Knights of the Cheese Wheel? Knights of the Glorious Something or Other? I remember reading about it in social studies. Maybe there was a group of knights that existed around that time. Maybe the words name the group he belongs to or something. Knights of the Poof! Or something. It's at least a place to start."

Angela looked up at me, her mouth open. "Q, that's actually a really good idea."

"I have them on occasion," I said.

"Have what on occasion?" Agent Callaghan opened the door just in time to hear me.

"Ideas," I said.

"Great. Have any ideas on where Buddy is going to show up?" he said.

"Uh. No . . . Not right now," I said. So lame. But Agent Callaghan had interrupted us right in the middle of a Boone conversation, and I couldn't think of anything intelligent to say.

"Well, if anything comes to either of you, speak up. You're both pretty smart. Ideas are welcome," he said. He reached into the bag of stuff he'd brought and handed us both a bottled water and—a Kit Kat bar.

I stared at him, mouth open. Couldn't be sure if he was making a joke or not.

"I figured since you didn't get to finish the one earlier . . ." he said.

"Oh, man," I said.

"Q . . ."Angela warned me. She was getting as bad as Roger.

"Whaffft?" I said, as I jammed pieces of chocolate paradise into my mouth. Since the entire bar was gone in about three seconds, she had no time to say anything else.

"You're disgusting," she said.

"Maybe, but it sure tastes better than toe-feet or fu-tot or whatever we have to eat."

"It's tofu and you know it. My dad is going—oh no, you don't," she said. I was grabbing for her candy bar. I figured since she wasn't going to eat it . . .

"Hypocrite," I said.

"I'm saving it for later," she said. But she sounded guilty about it, whereas I couldn't care less. What was Roger going to do if he caught me eating junk food, send me to boarding school? Oh, wait.

"Don't worry, Q," Agent Callaghan said from the front seat. "I brought more Kit Kats and plenty of other snacks. I suggest you get comfortable. Stakeouts can be long and boring."

He was right about the boring part. After about ten minutes, I was losing my mind. I couldn't sit still. I reached into my pocket for a deck of cards.

"Don't even think about it," Angela whispered– menacingly, I might add. She had the same look on her face as she had when she kicked Eben in the head back in Philadelphia.

I was stuck. Another five minutes passed. I drank one bottle of water and tried a game of license-plate alphabet on the cars that passed by. I got to D before I gave up. Clearly, I was not cut out for surveillance.

"Um. Agent Callaghan? Can I have another one of those Kit Kat bars?"

He reached in the bag and tossed one to me. I snatched it out of the air. While Angela shook her head, I ate the entire bar in seven bites. The way things were going, Roger would be sending us to a boarding school that only served bean sprouts.

It would be just my luck.

Buddy's Back

Buddy T. waited patiently for the assistant bank manager to leave the small room so he could open his safe-deposit box. It had been a nightmare getting back to the West Coast. Once he'd disposed of the van and his associate, he'd boarded a train and headed west. He couldn't believe how long it took to get anywhere by train these days. The trip was interminably long, and the food was terrible. There were delays, stops and starts, and more delays. Each time the train stopped he was fairly certain he spotted plainclothes U.S. Marshals slowly walking through each car. Whenever they did, he somehow managed to avoid their interest.

Once he arrived in San Francisco, he'd retrieved his numerous fake IDs from one of the several safe houses he owned in the Bay Area. He worried about the surveillance footage at the John Hancock building. He and his team had worn hats and done their best to keep their heads down to avoid cameras. And so far the news media had reported no suspects in relation to the attack that had been thwarted in

Chicago. That didn't mean they didn't have any. They were just keeping it quiet.

Buddy flipped open the lid of the safe-deposit box. Inside were several shrink-wrapped stacks of bills. He loaded them into his backpack. He was wearing jeans, a baseball cap, sunglasses, and a brown jacket. When he left the bank, he'd look like a regular guy. No one would ever guess he was carrying thousands of dollars.

It would take him a day or two to hit all the banks to pick up the "rest of his life" money, jewels, and securities. Then he planned to disappear. He had not heard from Number One since the attacks. Truthfully, that scared him more than any manhunt that might be in place searching for him. The longer he didn't hear from Number One, the more nervous he became.

Focus, he thought. Number One had a way of showing up unexpectedly. Buddy wanted to get his stuff and get out. He grabbed the bag and headed for the door.

Done with his business in the bank, he squinted in the sunshine as he stepped outside. This section of the Mission District was busy, and the sidewalks were crowded. He had parked his car across the street. As he strode into the crosswalk, a dark panel van screeched to a halt directly in front of him.

The side door flew open, and two men leaped out. One of them quickly put a Taser to Buddy's neck. Buddy felt his body convulse and then turn to rubber. He slumped toward the ground, but the two men lifted him effortlessly into the van. The door slammed shut.

It sped away, its tires screaming as they dug into the pavement.

Aroma

Aside from the fact that the coach could carry all of them, it was not a good vehicle for driving or surveillance, especially in a city like San Francisco. It certainly wasn't unobtrusive. It was also hard to maneuver.

Boone, Eben, and Malak sat in chairs at the table. Croc was curled up on the floor next to Boone. Malak stared down at the table, saying nothing. When the quiet lingered, Eben finally broke the ice.

"Is there any clue as to where Buddy might go first?" he asked. "Do any of the banks have larger deposits or have any of them made more offshore transactions than the others?"

"X-Ray said no," Boone said. "Pretty equal amounts on deposit. Equal number of transfers from each branch. They wouldn't make it that easy."

There were a few more minutes of silence as Ziv steered the coach through the city.

"I hope he shows up soon," Malak said. "I have many questions for Buddy T."

"With all the accounts he has access to, the way we know the cell is compartmentalized, he's at least its moneyman. If he's not Number Two, he must know who is. Or have a way of finding him," Boone said.

"But how do we find him? He has to know he was caught on security cameras carrying a chemical weapon into the Hancock building. He won't show up at his home," Eben said.

"X-Ray is looking for other houses, condos, and apartments based on the aliases he found attached to the bank records," Boone said. "But he could have used a whole other set of aliases for real estate transactions. But X-Ray will find a lead. He always does."

"And what do we do when we find him?" Malak asked.

"I think we use the Leopard," he said.

"What do you mean?"

Ziv spoke up from the driver's seat. "You were set up. Three of their council of five died shortly after meeting with you. The media has reported that the attack in Chicago was foiled. If the attack had succeeded, you would have been a casualty. But it failed. Now they know the Leopard is on the hunt. She will want her revenge. We will use that."

"Malak, listen," Boone said. "You've sacrificed so much already. If you want to sit this one out we can find Buddy T. without you. No one would blame you."

"No, Boone. I will not quit until we have destroyed them. It's the only way Angela will ever truly be safe."

Boone nodded.

"We are here," Ziv said. "This is as good a place as any to split up and cover the banks in this zone. We can keep the coach here as a base."

"All right," Boone said. "The other bank is three blocks north of here. Malak and Ziv, you go there; Eben and I will go to the one south." He took out a small plastic bag filled with the tiny earbuds X-Ray created. They were made of clear plastic, were wireless, and sat inside the ear, making them ideal for surveillance.

"Everyone check your weapons. We can't each stay on one bank for too long. I'm certain the cell is trailing Buddy or running countersurveillance. They'll be sure to spot us. So meet back here in thirty minutes." Boone picked up a duffel bag from the passenger seat. "I've got different hats, sunglasses, and other stuff in here," he said. "We'll change up our appearance and then move on to the next banks on the list until we find him. Any questions?"

Ready for their operation, the four of them left the coach and headed out into the city streets.

That Was Odd

"Whoa!" Agent Callaghan shouted from the front seat. I was slumped in the backseat, busy practically crawling out of my skin from boredom. But his shout got my attention and I straightened myself out so I could sit up.

"What? What is it?" Angela said.

"It's Buddy T. He's right here!"

"Where?" I said. I was still scrambling, trying to sit up and look out the front windshield.

"Angela," Callaghan shouted, "get Boone on the phone. Tell him to get Felix and Uly . . . What the—"

I finally spotted Buddy T. He was disguised in jeans, ball cap, and sunglasses, not his usual suit and tie. But there was no doubt. It was Buddy. He was carrying a small duffel bag.

As he stepped into the crosswalk, a van screeched to a halt right beside him. Two guys wearing black fatigues, both of them looking like 'roided-up weightlifters, barreled out of the van. One used a Taser on Buddy. *Way to go, Taser guy!* I thought. Then the two men dragged him into the van, and it peeled away. Okay. That wasn't so good. We needed Buddy. We could hear the sound of squealing tires all the way down the street from where we were parked.

"Hang on!" Agent Callaghan shouted. He slammed the car into gear and it surged out onto the street. The van was already nearly out of sight and moving fast. Callaghan laid on the horn, whipping in and out of traffic.

Angela was fumbling in her backpack for her phone. She was saying something to me but I wasn't paying attention. That's because I was concentrating on willing Agent Callaghan to not get us into a five-car pileup. We were flying down the street. I knew Secret Service agents were probably highly trained drivers, but I felt like I was on a roller coaster that was completely off the rails.

As we were just about to cross the next intersection, a late-model blue sedan sped into the street, skidding to a stop right in front of us. We were going to crash.

"HANG ON!" Agent Callaghan shouted.

He hit the brakes and Angela and I hurtled forward in our seat belts, instinctively throwing our hands up and bracing them against the front seat. I don't know how he did it, but he stopped the car just a few inches short of the sedan.

Agent Callaghan put the car in reverse and turned, looking out through the back window. We twisted around to look with him and heard more squealing tires as a minivan braked to a stop behind us and blocked us in.

Then it got weird.

And by weird, I mean terrifying.

From the front car this old guy—and I mean, like, senior

citizen old–jumped out of the car. At first, I thought he was going to ask Agent Callaghan for his insurance information, until he pulled a giant gun from under his jacket.

"Get down!" Agent Callaghan shouted.

Before I could duck, movement through the rear window caught my eye. There was a little old lady with a big floppy hat and sunglasses standing outside the minivan. A scary, frightening little old lady in a floppy hat and sunglasses who just happened to be holding a huge machine pistol. But that was all I saw, because by that time, my seat belt was off and I was on the floor. I heard gunshots, exploding tires, and the sound of shattering glass. I closed my eyes. With all my might, I tried to *poof!* like I did in Chicago. But when I opened them, I was still in the backseat.

"Throw your cell phones out the window," someone said. "Now! Don't even move or we shoot the kids!"

It was quiet a moment. I was pretty sure Agent Callaghan was considering his options. I sincerely hoped he'd arrive at a decision that ended in us not getting shot.

"Do what they say," Agent Callaghan said from the front seat.

I jerked my phone out of my pants pocket and tossed it through the broken window. Angela and Callaghan followed suit. Someone outside must have stomped on them, because I heard the crunch of plastic and glass.

I expected more gunshots, but none came. It was quiet for a moment, then came the shrieking sound of tires on asphalt as the cars sped away.

"Angela! Q! Are you okay?"

"I will be after years of therapy!" I shouted.

"What happened?" Angela was the first of us to peek over the front seat. I was still busy cowering.

"They shot out the tires. The cell had eyes on Buddy. Somehow they were able to track him. They had a grab-and-go team and put two following teams in place with instructions to stop anyone who tried to follow when they snatched him," Callaghan said.

"What are we going to do?" Angela asked him.

"Right now we need to get out of here before the cops show up. We don't have time to answer questions. They'll trace the car to me, but I'll badge my way out of it later. Let's go."

We all climbed out of the car and ran past dozens of startled onlookers.

Number One

Buddy T. blinked, his bleary eyes trying to adjust to the bright light that bored into them. He still felt weak and rubbery from the Taser, his legs too feeble to stand. Slowly regaining consciousness, he discovered his arms and legs were bound to the chair he sat in. He couldn't move, even if he were able.

When he could focus, through his squinted eyes he saw a concrete floor, steel rafters, and not much else. He thought it must be a warehouse. It was hard to tell, because he couldn't see much beyond the light in front of him. The room had a high ceiling and it echoed like an empty space at first. But then he heard the click of heels on the floor behind the light. Faint, but someone was there.

"Hello?" he mumbled. He was still feeling the effects of the Taser and his tongue didn't want to work right.

There was no answer, but the pacing continued. After what seemed like hours, the person spoke.

"Buddy, Buddy, Buddy," the voice said. "What am I going to do with you?"

Buddy T. instantly recognized the gravelly voice and his heart sank. The mysterious pacing man was Number One. How could he have found him? He had been so careful.

Easy. He always finds you.

His head drooped. Though he tried not to show it, he was terrified.

"Where were you off to, Buddy T.?" Number One asked.

"I . . . what? Nowhere . . ." Buddy stammered.

"That isn't what it looked like, Buddy T."

"I don't . . . I wasn't going . . . you're mistaken."

"Am I mistaken, Buddy T.? Am I? Because I don't think I am."

Buddy found the repeated use of his name unnerving.

"You don't understand, I–"

His duffel bag came flying through the air from behind the light and landed, open, at his feet. The shrink-wrapped stacks of bills spilled out, scattering across the floor.

"I don't understand? I *understand* perfectly, Buddy T. You've been a bad boy. You're gathering up my money and planning on running off."

"No! Listen! I'm telling you . . . I knew after Chicago things would get hot. The Feds would be looking everywhere. I just wanted to take what I could get and hold it for you. In case they got on to us somehow."

"Now how could they get on to us, Buddy T.? Weren't you careful? You're just about the most careful guy I know."

"Of course. But the Feds have all kinds of ways to–"

"No! No, they don't. Not us! Never us, Buddy T. We're too wary. Too smart. We're the ghost cell, Buddy T. So what were you doing with the cash?"

"I wasn't . . . I . . ."

"No more lies, *partner.*"

Ever since Buddy had first met him, Number One had kept a unique and unusual public identity. But in private he was completely different. And scary. Buddy T. was not a brave man. He'd killed the cell member in Chicago and left the body behind in the burning van, just as Number One ordered him to. It was the first time he'd ever killed anyone. It made him vomit immediately. Right there in the dirt of the vacant lot. He was a moneyman. A manager. He made it possible for others to do the killing. That was how he served the cause. He killed from afar, not up close. Not until he'd shot the man in Chicago.

"I swear . . . I–"

"You know what, Buddy T.? It doesn't matter anymore. We are close now. I think you were planning to light out somewhere. Live on the beach, in a little hut. But I still need you, Buddy T. I have one last little job for you."

Buddy tried to stifle a groan. The last few weeks, ever since Number One had been escalating things, acting recklessly, all Buddy T. could think about was getting as far away from this man as possible. Now he felt as if he never would.

"What do you want me to do?"

"I need you to get something out of one of your hidey holes."

"What is it?"

"It's a steel box about two feet long, maybe eight or ten inches wide. I gave it to you years ago, a while after you and

I first partnered up. I need it right away. How soon can you get it?"

Buddy racked his brain, trying to remember the box. He could not.

"I . . . don't . . . I can't remember. You've given me so much stuff over the years. I've got dozens of safe-deposit boxes—"

"Think, Buddy T.," Number One interrupted. "Think real hard."

The beads of perspiration trickling down his face turned into a sweat tsunami, as drops of it now rushed down his face in waves.

"I don't know! I swear! It could be anywhere."

Number One was silent for a moment. There was no sound except the tap, tap, tap of his boots on the floor. Then he stepped forward, his face still hidden by the light, but all Buddy saw were the pointed toes of his cowboy boots sticking out of the shadows. Number One always wore cowboy boots of some kind.

"All right, here is how it's going to be. My boys are coming in here in a minute and turn you loose. Then they're going to take you to every bank on your list until you find that box. If you're holding out on me? If you don't find it? Well, you ever see anybody fall off the Golden Gate Bridge?"

"No," Buddy croaked, closing his eyes, his head sagging toward his chest.

"In this case it *is* the fall that kills you, Buddy T. You see, from that high up, when you hit the water? It's like hitting concrete. But you know what will be different about your fall?"

Buddy was too frightened to speak. He could only shake

his head.

"What'll be different is, you'll be dead before you hit the water. Because before my boys toss you over the side? They'll cut your throat first."

Buddy could not help it. A miserable, pitiful sob escaped his lips.

"Buck up, Buddy T. That's how the ghost cell rolls, my man! Heck, you knew that when you signed on."

Buddy heard a weird noise. A slight swooshing sound, like something zooming through the air at a high rate of speed. He couldn't be sure, but he could practically swear that Number One was no longer in the room. It was almost like he'd vanished into thin air.

All Buddy could do was wait to be set free.

Hot Pursuit

Boone rapped on the door of the coach with the pointed toe of one of his cowboy boots. One hand held a cardboard tray full of coffees, and the other carried a bag of bagels. They were parked in a side lot off Market Street, across and down from one of the banks on X-Ray's list. Boone had gone to get food. Stakeouts could take hours, if not days, and he wanted to make sure everyone stayed as fresh as possible.

"Somebody open up! Hurry!" he called out.

Eben opened the door. Boone bounded up the steps.

"You were gone quite a while," Malak said. Ever since she'd arrived at the hangar, Boone had picked up on the fact that she was suspicious of him. In some ways he didn't blame her. In her place, he'd probably feel the same way. There was nothing he could do about it now.

"Long line at the Starbucks," he said. He put the coffee and bagels on the table. Eben pulled one from the bag and put it to his nose, inhaling deeply. A big smile crossed his face.

"Would you two like a moment alone?" Boone asked.

"No," Eben said, taking a large bite from the bagel. "But Eben Lavi does not eat weeds. Not on a stakeout. Have you seen the refrigerator? Nothing but greens and other strange gelatinous materials of suspicious origin."

"Yeah, well. Drink up, grab something to eat. Pick out something from the duffel to change up your look. We don't have a lot of time. We've got to get back out–"

Boone's phone chirped. The screen read: "Unknown Caller."

"Hello?"

"Boone! It's me. Angela."

"Angela?" Boone said. He put the phone on speaker.

"We found Buddy. I mean we saw him. He's gone now. But we spotted him, coming out of a bank."

"Did Pat grab him?" Boone said.

"No," Angela said. Boone thought she sounded out of breath.

"Angela, are you all right?" Malak cut in. She heard the same thing in Angela's voice.

"Yes, but we . . . we lost our car. And, um . . . our phones."

"What? What do you mean you lost your car? Where's Pat? What's going on?" Malak stood. She was trying to keep herself under control. But the stress in her voice and stance was evident.

"Agent Callaghan is right here. When Buddy T. came out of the bank, somebody in a van kidnapped him. When we tried to follow, two cars cut us off, and we were stuck."

Boone looked at Malak.

"Angela, are you all right? Is anyone hurt?" Malak

asked her.

"No, we're fine, it happened a while ago. First we hopped a cab to get away and make sure we weren't being followed. Then we had to find a place to get a burner phone so we could call. We're waiting to get on a bus to make sure there's no countersurveillance. Agent Callaghan says to wait until he's certain we aren't being followed before someone picks us up, but he's pretty sure we're clear. But anyway, Buddy T. was taken in a black panel van. We didn't get a plate number," she said.

"That's okay, honey. You did fine," Malak said.

"Angela, hang on a second," Boone cut in. "I'm going to conference in X-Ray." He punched a couple buttons on the phone and X-Ray answered.

"X, it's Boone. Pat and his team spotted Buddy T. at their bank in the Mission District. But a backup crew took out their vehicle. Get into the traffic cams in the area. You're looking for a black panel van. Find it."

"I'm on it," X-Ray said.

"Angela, where are you guys now?" Boone asked.

Angela gave him the cross streets.

"Okay, listen—" he began, but his line beeped. Uly was calling. Boone hit another button to add him to the conference call.

"Hey, Boone, guess who just showed up at our bank?" Uly asked.

"Buddy."

"Yep. In a black panel van. And he's got a couple of friends with him. Looks like hired muscle. What do you want us to do?"

Boone thought for a second. Two teams had sealed off Pat, Angela, and Q from following. That was in addition to the team that grabbed Buddy. It was a good bet the cell had a similar setup here.

"Okay. Do not, repeat, do not let Buddy T. leave that bank. I'm sure you guys can handle the two goons in the van. But look around for a second team or even a third team. Somebody snatched Buddy right off the street in front of Pat. When Pat tried to follow the van, two other crews took out their vehicle. So stay alert. Find their backup and take them out first if you get the opportunity. Pat is closest to you, so I'm going to have him hop a cab. He'll be there in minutes. We're rolling your way now. X-Ray, did you get all that?"

"Copy," X-Ray said.

"Get inside the cameras in that bank vault as soon as you can. We need to find out what Buddy's after. Angela, give the phone to Pat," Boone said.

Boone looked around. Ziv started the coach and pulled onto the street. Malak's face was taut with worry and anger.

"It's me, Boone," Pat said.

"Get a cab and get to Uly and Felix as fast as you can. I got a feeling they're going to need backup. But be sure you stash Angela and Q someplace close by but safe. We're on our way."

"We'll be there in ten minutes," Pat said. He disconnected Angela's phone.

"X-Ray, Uly, you guys clear on what you're supposed to do?" Boone asked.

"Copy," X-Ray said. "I'll send a link to your phone as soon as I'm in the system."

"Roger that, Boone," Uly said. "We got this."

Boone disconnected the phone. Malak glared at him.

"I know," Boone said. "But you heard me. Pat will put them someplace safe. I'm sure they'll be perfectly fine."

Running Out of Numbers

Buddy T. stepped out of the van. Neither of Number One's men said anything, but the one on the driver's side sneered as he racked the slide on his machine pistol. It sent a clear message.

To Buddy, the walk from the van to the bank felt as if he were passing through a tunnel that was collapsing around him. On the drive over he had tried to remember the box Number One described. He couldn't. Over the years Number One had given him an unbelievable number of things to store. Paintings, sculptures, and other works of art, not to mention all kinds of currency, gold and silver, jewels, bonds, stocks, and securities. There was an insane amount of money behind the ghost cell.

Once inside the bank, an assistant manager took him to the vault. Buddy felt so paralyzed with fear it was almost like he was seeing himself sleepwalk through a dream. He watched as the young man in his Brooks Brothers suit unlocked the box with the bank key. He was barely able to get his own key in the other lock.

"Do you need help, sir?" the manager asked.

"What? Oh. No. I can take it from here . . . thank you," Buddy mumbled. This box was one of the bigger models, made to hold large objects, and it had a smaller metal box inside it. Buddy lifted the lid and looked at the contents. There was a manila envelope full of bonds, dozens of gold coins in plastic storage boxes, and more shrink-wrapped cash. He dug through everything, trying to find the object Number One had described. It wasn't there. He groaned in dismay.

Buddy paced back and forth in the empty vault as he considered his options. He could try to sneak out of the bank, but that was unlikely to work. Even if he went through a rear door or emergency exit, he was sure there were more than just the two goons out front watching him. He wouldn't get far. Number One had eyes everywhere.

Buddy ran his hands across his forehead. It was soaked in sweat. He had been a fool to think he could outwit Number One. As always, the man had been a step ahead of him the whole time.

After more pacing back and forth, he reached into the box, grabbing a few of the gold coins and shoving them into his pockets. He tore open one of the shrink-wrapped packs of cash and stuffed several thousand dollars into his pockets. He was going to run for it. What other choice did he have?

Unless.

There might be someone who could help him out of this, if the rumors about him were true. It just might be his only option. He pulled out his cell phone and scrolled through his contacts and found the number he was looking for. His finger shook as he pushed the call button.

"Howdy, Buddy," Boone said. "What's your number?"

"Boone? What . . . who? What do you mean?" Boone had caught Buddy completely off guard. "My telephone number? What are you talking about?"

"Well, Buddy, I just wanted to know if you were Number One or Number Two? Numbers Three through Five are dead. I figure you're running out of numbers. Personally, I'm bettin' on you being Number Two. Because to tell the truth, Buddy, I just don't see you smart enough to be the Number One of anything, let alone the ghost cell."

"I . . . don't know . . . what you're talking about," Buddy said.

"Okay, Buddy. Whatever you say. Good-bye."

"No! Boone! Wait! Don't hang up!"

There was silence on the other end.

"Boone? Boone? Please don't hang up. I . . . we need to talk."

"I'm listening," Boone finally said.

"I can . . . there's stuff . . . I need." This had been a bad idea. Buddy couldn't get the words out.

"All right, Buddy, let me ask you a question."

"What?"

"How much cash and gold you got in that safe-deposit box you're standing next to?"

"What? I don't—"

"How much did you just jam in your pockets?"

"How? . . . where . . ." Buddy looked around and saw the

security camera in the corner of the vault.

"Are you watching me?"

"Yup."

"How? There aren't supposed to be cameras in safe deposit-box vaults. It's supposed to be private."

"Nothing's private anymore, Buddy. Not since you and your terrorist buddies started acting up on 9/11. Now. Tell me who Buddy T. really is."

"I . . . I'm Number Two. I'm in trouble."

"Oh, you have no idea how much trouble you're in, Buddy."

"No, I mean—I know . . . but you want to destroy the ghost cell, right? I can give you Number One. But I want things."

"I want things too, Buddy. So far you haven't given me anything."

"I will tell you what he wants! And I can set it up for you to catch him when he comes to get it."

"What does he want?"

"A box."

"What's in it?"

"I have no idea."

"Buddy . . ."

"No! Boone, I really mean it. He's crazy. He's got millions, maybe hundreds of millions in cash and gold and art, and he just wants this one box. He said he gave it to me years ago for safekeeping. I don't remember it. He's given me so much stuff over the years. I'm sure I have it stored somewhere. I just don't remember where."

"So why don't you just find it and give it to him? Why are

you calling me?"

"Well, Boone, in case you forgot, apparently you're following me. And so is he. And he has people outside the bank waiting. And I'm more scared of him than I am of you."

"Is that right? I don't think it's going to work, Buddy. Not unless you tell me who he is first. I mean, suppose we show up and take out the guys outside the bank? Your Number One is going to get suspicious and just disappear. You need to tell me who he is now. Before you leave the bank."

"No way, Boone. I'm not stupid. I tell you who he is without some guarantees, I'm dead anyway. I want full immunity and witness protection."

Buddy held his phone away from his ear at the sound of Boone's laughter.

"Immunity? Buddy, you'll be lucky if you don't get the death penalty."

Now, despite his circumstances, Buddy was getting angry.

"Really, Boone? Then you'll never find him. You'll never stop him. So you've taken out some of the cell's top leadership. Congratulations. But he'll just rebuild. And start all over. That what you want?"

"Good-bye, Buddy. Have fun trying to outrun the guys outside the bank."

"Boone, listen! We can make a deal! I can give you everything! You think if you help me out he'll disappear? I don't think so. He's crazier than I've ever seen him. And that's pretty whacked. I think—no, I know—he really, really wants this box. And I have no idea what's even in it. You take out the guys out front, pick me up, and we can fake it until I find the box. Then we set up a meet, and you get him."

There were several seconds of silence. To Buddy, each one lasted several eternities.

"Boone?"

"All right, Buddy. Help is on the way. You stay inside that vault. One of my guys will come in and get you. After they take out your friends outside. They're big, well trained, and, as a special bonus, they don't like you. You try to run and you'll just upset them."

"Okay. Okay. Whatever. I'll wait."

"Good boy, Buddy. Sit tight. Help is on the way."

Start Spreading the News

Felix and Uly sat in the Range Rover. Felix was scanning the street with a small pair of binoculars. Uly checked his pistol and pulled two pairs of flex-cuffs from a duffel bag on the floor behind the passenger seat. Felix put the binoculars in the glove box and checked his own pistol.

"What are they doing?" Uly asked.

"Nothing I can see. They're just sitting there, fidgeting and talking to each other. Probably wondering what's taking Buddy so long," Felix said.

"I don't see any backup anywhere. Do you?" Uly asked.

"Nope. If they're here, they must be invisible. Maybe they don't have a backup crew. It is just Buddy, after all. Those two look like they could handle him pretty easy."

"Could be," Uly said. "But you know what Boone always says."

"Uh, no. Howdy?" Felix was confused.

"No. 'There's always backup.' "

"I've never heard him say that," Felix said.

"He does."

"But sometimes there is no backup. Why would he say that?"

"Because he's Boone. He likes to speak in riddles. How you wanna play this?"

"I was thinking 'drunken preacher man.' I'll stagger up the sidewalk and approach on the passenger-side window. You come up along the driver's side and take him out while they're both focused on me. I get the guy riding shotgun. Sound good?" Felix asked.

"Why do you get to be 'drunken preacher man'?" Uly complained.

"Because I'm a better actor than you."

"What? No you aren't!"

"Yes, I am," Felix said. "I did some security work in Hollywood a few years back. Everybody said I was a natural."

"A natural crackpot," Uly muttered. "Let's do this."

They climbed out of the Ranger Rover and stretched a little, pulling their jackets over their holstered weapons. Felix nodded at Uly and started up the sidewalk. He staggered back and forth, stumbling along. People on the street gave him a wide berth.

"Hallelujah!" he shouted. "It's a glorious day."

Uly had to admit Felix made a pretty convincing drunken preacher. Uly's jacket had the pocket liners cut out so that he could put his hand in his pocket and reach his pistol.

Felix arrived at the van. The windows were down. He leaned over and put his forearms on the door and peered through the opening. Both of the men inside turned to look at him. Uly quickened his pace toward the driver's-side window.

"Sh'ello, boyss. Do you have a moment to hear the—"

"Beat it, freak," the thug in the passenger seat said.

"Hey! Tha's not nice," Felix complained. He closed one eye and squinted at the two men as if he were trying hard to focus.

Now Uly was in position.

"I said beat—"

But he never got the chance to finish because Felix reached in and grabbed the back of his neck. With great force, he jammed it forward, smashing the thug's forehead on the dashboard. As the driver was reaching for his pistol, Uly grabbed him by the hair and, repeating his partner's maneuver, smashed him face first into the steering wheel. They threw open the doors and dragged the stunned men out of the front seat and held them up against the van with one hand while patting them down with the other. Each suspect was searched and the flex-cuffs were on in seconds. They each took their woozy man by the arm and prepared to lead the men back down the street to the Ranger Rover.

"Wait!" Uly said. And Felix stopped dead in his tracks.

"What?" Felix asked.

"Your chest . . . look," Uly said. Confused, Felix looked down and saw that the bright red dot from a sniper rifle's laser-targeting system had appeared on his chest. An identical mark hovered directly over Uly's heart.

"Oops," Felix said.

"There's always backup," Uly said.

Not Staying Put

Riding in a cab in San Francisco is a unique experience. I don't recommend it. Ever. Sure, I suppose there are some San Francisco cabbies out there who don't drive like each block is his own demolition derby, but I have yet to meet one. If you have "riding in a cab in San Francisco" on your bucket list, you can just skip it. Cross it off and move on to wrestling an alligator.

Of course it didn't help that when we jumped into the cab, Agent Callaghan flashed his Secret Service credentials and told the cabbie to get to the bank "and don't worry about the lights or tickets." As we careened in and out of traffic, I had both hands pressed firmly against the back of the front seat. Which totally grossed me out. Because I didn't want to think about the variety of things that had been spilled, spewed, or otherwise expelled on the back of that seat. Could it be worse than pigeon poop? Probably. Note to self: add hand sanitizer to cargo pants at earliest opportunity. And a barf bag. Being a spy has given me a very sensitive stomach, what with all the shooting and the *poofing!* and the careening.

"There they are!" Angela shouted.

"Pull over!" Agent Callaghan shouted at the cabbie. The driver whipped the wheel hard to the right and slipped into a no-parking zone. We clambered out and he sped off before he even got paid. I think having a Secret Service agent in the car made him nervous. I didn't blame him.

"Why aren't they moving?" I said. And it was true. Felix and Uly were about fifty yards down the street with two guys in flex-cuffs next to the black van. But everyone was standing still.

"Something's wrong," Agent Callaghan said. He studied the rooftops on the other side of the street. I followed his eyes but I didn't see anything.

"Sniper?" Angela said.

"That'd be my guess," he said. I was about to ask her how she knew that when I remembered she probably had already memorized the entire *How to Be a Secret Service Agent* handbook. Of course she would know to look for snipers. That was messed up. What kind of fifteen-year-old girl walks around looking for places where a sniper might set up shop? Oh yeah. Angela.

Agent Callaghan must have been thinking the same thing because he was studying every building on the street. About twenty yards down the sidewalk toward the van was a diner. It didn't look like a place that would win any food awards. But I knew what was coming next.

"Listen to me very carefully. Uly and Felix are pinned down by a sniper team. I know where they are and I'm going to take them out. You two are going into that diner and wait there. If I don't come back, you go out the back door. Head straight to your parents' hotel," he said, pulling a wad of bills out of his pocket and handing it to Angela.

"We can help," Angela said. "Create a diversion or—"

"No! *Absolutely not.* You wait. If things go south you *get out.* I'm not messing around. Do you understand me?"

"Yes," we both said at the same time.

"Good. Now go."

We strolled casually up the street and went into the diner. Of course Angela wanted a seat right by the window. I would have preferred a safer location. Like a diner in South Dakota. I doubted the ghost cell was interested in attacking South Dakota. We watched as Agent Callaghan quickly crossed the street and disappeared down an alley.

A waitress brought us waters and menus. Despite my best efforts my stomach involuntarily growled. Maybe we had enough time for a cheeseburger before we had to start running for our lives. Angela was staring out the window and biting her lip.

"What?" I said. When she did the lip-biting thing, Angela had something she wanted to say. It was her tell.

"I don't like this," she said.

"Really? You don't enjoy being terrified and surrounded by thugs and terrorists with guns all the time? Because I *love* it."

"No. It's not that. I don't like this specific situation."

"Why?"

"Remember when we saw Buddy at the bank earlier?"

"No. I'm trying to completely repress that memory. The

old lady in the floppy hat with a pistol the size of an anvil who shot out our tires is freaking me out."

"There are snipers. They've got Uly and Felix pinned down. Buddy is in the bank. It's a standoff."

"I'm sure Agent Callaghan will figure it out."

"I know. But at the first bank, they had *three* teams. What if they have three teams here? I mean, now that they have Buddy, wouldn't they put even more guys on him, to make sure something doesn't go wrong? So, if the guys in the van are *one* team and the snipers are the *second* team, where is the *third*? What if Callaghan takes out the snipers on the roof and then the third team shoots Uly and Felix?"

I hadn't thought about that. I liked Felix and Uly. They were cool. Plus they were big. And strong. Both of them could break things. They shot back at people who were shooting at us. All the time. I didn't want anything bad happening to them.

Angela was studying the street. The waitress came back and asked if we wanted anything.

"Cheeseburger. Fries. Chocolate shake."

"Q, how can you think of food at a time like this?"

"Angela, A, I'm a thirteen-year-old boy. News flash. I'm *always* thinking about food. B, Agent Callaghan ordered us to stay put. So I might as well eat. I need my strength."

Angela rolled her eyes and told the waitress she was fine with her water.

"You're an animal," I said.

She didn't respond. She was observing the street. Her eyes went everywhere and I knew she was looking for anyone who looked like they might be part of the ghost cell.

"I wish Boone would get here," she muttered.

"I'm sure they're on the way."

Her eyes went back to the street. I didn't see anything strange. It looked like a regular San Francisco street. Business people, tourists, the homeless, and street performers lined both sides of it and all of them hustled about, trying to get wherever they were going.

"Q?"

"Yes?"

"Look across the street in the doorway of that thrift shop right next to the bank entrance. There's a clown playing a banjo."

I looked. I didn't want to look because clowns freak me out. But sure enough, there was a poorly made-up, disheveled-looking clown, wearing an ill-fitting, stringy-haired orange wig and sitting cross-legged on the sidewalk with his back against the building near the thrift shop door. He was plucking at the banjo—but was he really watching Felix and Uly?

"I see him. How do you know he's not just a regular street performer?"

"I don't think so," Angela said.

"Why?"

"For one thing, he's watching Felix and Uly. He's trying not to stare at them but he keeps looking their way every few seconds. Second, most street musicians have their instrument case open so people can toss in cash. His case is closed."

"Maybe he's just playing for his art," I said. But I knew what she was thinking.

"Or maybe he's the backup and his banjo case is hiding a gun."

"What do we do?" I asked. "If you're right and we try to warn Felix and Uly, he starts shooting. Agent Callaghan is on a rooftop somewhere above him. He's probably not going to be able to take him out from up there. He's covered by that awning."

"We take him out," Angela declared quietly.

"*What?* No! This isn't funny, Angela," I whispered, because other customers in the diner were beginning to stare at us.

"Do you want Felix and Uly to get shot? He's sitting down. If we do it right, I can take him out with one tae kwan do kick before he gets to his feet. But we have to create some kind of distraction first. Some way of getting in between him and Uly."

I looked down at the table. The waitress had left the menu. It was covered in thick plastic and folded in thirds. I grabbed it and stood up.

"I have an idea. Let's go," I said, heading for the door.

"Wait. What's your idea?" She was hurrying to keep up.

"Simple. Magic."

The Hand (or the Foot) Is Quicker Than the Eye

They call it three-card monte. It's a common card game played by con men and street hustlers. Sometimes it's called find the lady because you use three cards—the two red jacks and the queen of hearts. The game involves getting unsuspecting people—what con men call "marks"—to bet on where the queen is after you shuffle the three cards. Like all card and magic tricks, it relies on sleight of hand, misdirection, and deception.

When we left the restaurant—after assuring the angry waitress we'd be coming back for our food and giving her ten dollars—we crossed the street. I was nervous and taking deep breaths. I had to be calm to pull this off. Sleight of hand doesn't work if your hands are shaking.

"I need some of the money Agent Callaghan gave you. Small bills," I said.

"What are you doing?" But she pulled a wad of cash from her pocket and handed it to me.

"You said we need a distraction. I'm going to distract. You're going to tae kwan do."

I hoped Angela was right. It would be a horrible shame if she clobbered an innocent clown. On second thought, there are no innocent clowns. So we were probably good either way.

"How?"

"Like I said, magic."

Everything seemed to slow down as we approached the clown. He was almost directly across from where Uly and Felix were standing still as stones beside the black van. I know it had only been a few minutes since we'd arrived on the scene but it felt like hours. Felix and Uly had these two guys in flex-cuffs and were talking to them in low voices. Everybody passing on the street probably assumed they were cops interrogating suspects. No one appeared to be paying attention. Except the evil clown.

I was also pretty sure Uly and Felix recognized us and knew we were there. But they were too well trained to acknowledge us. If they did, it might tip off the second crew (or even worse, the clown) that Felix and Uly's backup had arrived. Angela had slipped on a big pair of sunglasses. I had put on the ball cap and shades I always carried in my cargo shorts. Like spies, we had altered our appearance. We were running out of time before people started stopping to watch Felix and Uly or real cops showed up. And that might get a lot of people hurt.

As we got closer, I could hear the sound of the banjo. It was terrible. He was definitely a fake clown. No one could play the banjo that badly on purpose. A fake, malevolent, criminal, terrorist-assisting clown. Somebody had to take him down.

There was a wire trash can a few feet away. I grabbed it

and dragged it over so it was right between the clown and the Range Rover. I unfolded the plastic-laminated menu over the top of the trashcan so I had a portable tabletop to work on.

"Once I get going, keep an eye on Mr. Giggles with the banjo," I whispered to Angela. "And if you see a cop anywhere, give a shout. This is highly illegal. Don't want to cause a ruckus that might put Uly and Felix in danger."

With everything in place, I whipped out one of my decks and quickly found the three cards I needed. I started shuffling them back and forth.

"Step right up! Who feels lucky? Find the queen and win!" I shouted.

I whipped the cards back and forth, my hands a blur. There is a reason three-card monte is almost impossible to win. While the dealer is shuffling the cards, he's always holding two cards in one hand and one in the other. The trick is in the hand with two cards. When you first pick up the queen, you do it with the hand holding two cards. The mark will always think they're "following" the card in your hand.

Talking constantly to the crowd, you move the cards back and forth between hands, so you can toss either the top or bottom card onto your tabletop when you lay the three cards out. If you're good, the move is almost impossible to detect. The mark thinks they're keeping an eye on the queen, but they invariably pick the wrong card. Once in a while the mark gets lucky and picks the right card. Usually the dealer is working with a partner, whom he tips off to the correct location of the queen. They place a winning bet so it looks legit to the marks. I didn't have time to train Angela. I was going to have to hope

I was really good and nobody got lucky. Or Angela took out the clown soon.

"Who's a winner? Step right up! Find the queen!" I hollered to the passing crowd. Why was it taking Agent Callaghan so long to take out those snipers? Of course, I would imagine taking out snipers is not easy or something you can do really quickly. Because of all the guns.

No one was gathering. I nodded at Angela.

"How about you, young lady? Take a chance! Win money!" I shouted.

Angela stepped up and put a ten-dollar bill down on the menu.

"We have a player. Here we go. Watch closely. Where's the queen?"

I shuffled and shuffled, then I laid out the cards. As I withdrew my hands, I very quickly pointed to which card was the queen with my pinkie finger.

"Where is it? Where's the queen?" I shouted.

Angela pointed and I turned over the card, revealing the queen.

"Winner, winner, chicken dinner!" I called out, pulling a ten-dollar bill from my pocket and waving it around in the air before I handed it to her.

That got attention. When other people see or hear someone winning money, they get interested. It works every time. A couple of people stopped to watch.

"Who wants to win? Who wants to win? Place your bets and find the queen."

The gathering crowd was the trick. It was obscuring the

clown's view of Uly and Felix.

"Hey, kid," the clown spoke up from his spot on the sidewalk. "This is my turf. Beat it."

I ignored him.

"Who's going to be the next winner?" I said, furiously shuffling the cards back and forth.

A middle-aged guy wearing a ball cap that said "IOWA" on the brim put down ten dollars.

"Don't do it, Harold," his wife said, pulling at his arm. "It's a scam."

"It's no scam at all, everybody has a chance to win!" I shouted.

The clown spoke up again.

"Hey, kid. I want you out of here! This is my spot!"

I still ignored him and kept shuffling.

"Hey!" He put down the banjo. As he started to rise to his feet, Angela made her move. She faded out of the crowd around me and, quick as a cat, she darted across the sidewalk, launching a kick that landed right in his chest. It drove him back into the wall of the thrift shop. Stunned, he slumped back to the ground. For good measure, Angela grabbed him by the ears, pulled his head forward, and drove it hard back into the wall. The clown flopped forward, unconscious. Angela pushed him up into a sitting position and put the banjo back in his lap. He looked like just another passed-out street person.

I handed the money back to the man and folded up the menu.

"Sorry, gotta go," I said. I glanced at Uly and Felix, who were now looking up at the roof above us. They gave a little salute to someone up there. Agent Callaghan must have succeeded. They put the guys they'd cuffed in the back of the Range Rover. Uly stayed put while Felix went inside the bank.

Angela and I raced back to the restaurant. I hoped Agent Callaghan didn't see us sprinting across the street. When we returned to our table, the waitress brought my cheeseburger and I devoured it in about six bites. Angela was busy stealing my fries when Agent Callaghan returned.

"We got him," he said. "Let's go."

Tangled Webs

As we walked outside, the coach was pulling up in the street outside the bank. We hustled over and climbed inside. Angela went straight to her mom and they hugged again. Malak ran her hand over Angela's face, brushing her bangs away.

"Mom," Angela said. "I'm so glad to see you."

"I'm happy to see you, too, sweetheart."

I was pleased for Angela. There was still a lot of dangerous stuff ahead. But I couldn't help but think we were getting closer to the two of them finally being together. And it made me think about my mom and how I'd acted like a jerk about the whole boarding school thing. Seeing Malak and Angela together, I realized the lengths a parent would go to in order to protect his or her child. I thought about calling her right then. But Boone's cell phone beeped.

"Felix?" he said, answering the call. He listened for a few seconds. "All right. Tell him I'll be in in a minute. Malak, can you brief Pat, Angela, and Q while I'm inside?"

"Yes," Malak said. Boone quickly left the coach.

"Brief us about what?" Angela asked.

"When Buddy gets on the coach, I am morphing back into the Leopard. You and Q and Pat will have to pretend you do not know me—you have never met me," Malak said.

"Why?" Angela said, biting her lip.

"Because we can't trust Buddy. We know he's being watched. If Buddy should get away, or he's deceiving us or we're followed and the cell discovers a connection between us, then you would instantly become a target. And not only you, but Q, Roger, and Blaze. You would never be safe. We have it set up that I, as the Leopard, deduced that the cell planned to kill me in Chicago after the news got out about their failed weapon. And now, to exact my revenge, I have joined forces with Boone. I'm going to sweat Buddy and find out everything I can."

She looked out the window to see Buddy emerging from the bank. Boone had him by the arm. Felix walked behind him, one hand in his jacket pocket, glancing everywhere. The clown was still slumped in his spot. Angela must have really clocked him. Malak quickly slid into the passenger seat next to Ziv. Felix went to the clown and lifted him off the ground and slung him over his shoulder, picking up the banjo case with his free hand. He carried him to the Range Rover and he and Uly drove away with their passengers.

Boone wasn't gentle as he helped Buddy onto the bus. Ziv patted him down and found a ring of keys to a bunch of other safe-deposit boxes. He shoved Buddy into one of the chairs at the dining table. Buddy T. looked scared. Boone opened Buddy's duffel bag and spilled the contents onto the table.

There was cash, gold, and little felt bags that sounded like they were full of marbles as they crashed across the table.

"Wow, Buddy," Boone said. "The terrorism business must be good."

Buddy didn't say anything, but when he saw Angela and me he sneered. Even under duress, he couldn't help but be his usual obnoxious self.

"What are you two snots doing here?"

"There's still a tour, Buddy," Boone said. "I'm in charge of tour security. I couldn't very well let your pals in the cell get wind of me sending Q and Angela off someplace safe. If we did something unusual it might tip your buddies off."

Buddy didn't say anything, just stared sullenly at the floor.

"Plus as an extra added bonus. Yours ain't the only interesting call I've gotten lately. Have you met Anmar? Maybe you know her better by her nickname, the Leopard."

Buddy's head snapped up and his face went white as cotton. Malak slowly stood up from her spot in the shotgun seat. She took her time strolling back to where Buddy sat at the table. I couldn't help but notice how her entire persona had instantly changed. She moved and acted like a leopard. She *was* the Leopard.

To say Buddy was sweating now was like saying a typhoon is a little wet. Perspiration poured down his face and disappeared inside the collar of his shirt. Malak stood close to his chair, staring down at him, invading his personal space, scrutinizing him the way you might examine a wad of gum on the bottom of your shoe. Her reflexes were amazingly fast as she drew her pistol and placed the muzzle right against

Buddy's forehead.

Buddy made a little mewling noise.

"Anmar!" Boone said. But there was something in his voice. I could tell it was all rehearsed. They must have talked it over and planned what to do if they caught up with Buddy.

"Did you think you could *betray* me?" she said, her voice a whisper. It made her even scarier. I *knew* she was faking it and I was still terrified.

"I . . . wha . . . ah, Boone. Boone, make her go away," Buddy stammered.

"Nah," Boone said. He sat down at the other end of the table and leaned back in the chair, put his legs up, and crossed them at the ankles. "This is too much fun."

"This was *not* part of our deal," Buddy whined.

"Shut up. Stop whining," Malak hissed. "You sent me to Grant Park in Chicago. You were going to kill me and pin the attacks on me. That makes you my enemy, Mr. Buddy T. Do you know what happens to the Leopard's enemies?"

All of us were spellbound, watching what was going on with rapt attention. Ziv sat in the driver's seat, acting as if he was bored. But I was certain he was watching everything that moved outside. He'd probably seen this act from Anmar a thousand times.

"Boone . . . you promised . . ." Buddy whimpered.

Boone responded by reaching into his back pocket and pulling out a tattered paperback copy of *Moonraker*, a James Bond novel by Ian Fleming. He flipped it opened and started reading.

"So Boone and I have made a deal," Malak said. "For now

we are allies. You will help Boone with what he needs. You help him catch Number One. Or else you will answer to the Leopard. You will go to each bank until you find whatever it is Number One is looking for. If you don't cooperate, if you try to deceive us in any way, then Boone has agreed that you will be left to me," she said.

"Boone! This wasn't the deal."

Boone looked up from his book. "You expectin' a better offer, Buddy? Think maybe the president will walk on the coach here. Offer you a pardon?"

Buddy was silent a moment.

"Tell us who Number One is." Malak prodded him with the gun.

Buddy got a little spine at that point.

"No. No way. Kill me if you want, but until you have him locked up or me on an island somewhere with fifty armed guards, I am not saying another word about Number One. Not until I know he's off the board," Buddy said.

"You will speak or you will die," Malak said.

"No. I'm serious, Boone. You have no idea who you're dealing with. No matter what you do to me, he'll do worse. We made a deal. So either shoot me, or let's find what he's looking for."

The coach was silent for a moment.

"All right, Buddy. We'll do it your way. Anmar," Boone said. But she did not move. She held her gun firmly against Buddy's forehead.

"Anmar," Boone said, a warning tone in his voice.

Malak relaxed and returned the gun to its holster.

"Where do we start looking, Buddy? Where did they take you?"

"I don't know. When they grabbed me, I'm pretty sure they took me to a warehouse. But I don't know which one. We own a bunch of them. They blindfolded me when they took me back out. So it could be anywhere."

"Eben, put some cuffs on our friend Buddy here and let's put him in the bedroom with Croc," Boone said.

"What? No way, you're not putting me anywhere with that dog!" Buddy said.

But by then Eben had jerked Buddy to his feet and slipped flex-cuffs over his wrists, pulling them extra tight. He grabbed Buddy by the collar and pushed him toward the bedroom door. Croc followed along and slipped into the bedroom as Eben shoved Buddy inside and shut the door.

Boone stood up, his one arm across his chest and the other hand on his chin. He was silent a moment. He called X-Ray.

"X, cross-reference any industrial or commercial real estate locations with the list of aliases you found on the bank accounts. See if you get any hits," he said. We all waited a few minutes, not saying anything. Bringing Buddy onto the coach had made everyone tense. At least it made me tense.

"Got it," Boone finally said. "Send me the addresses. And while you're at it–I've got extra phones here for Q and Angela–get them set up and cloned to their old ones in case their parents call." Boone opened a drawer on the coach and handed Angela and me new iPhones.

"Okay," he said. "We'll split up. Pat, Angela, and Q will come with me. X and Vanessa will follow in the intellimobile.

The rest of you will go with Buddy to the banks. We need to find this thing that Number One wants. While you all do that, we'll look for the warehouse where they held Buddy. Probably won't find anything even if we do locate it but it's our only lead to Number One. I've got Everett and a couple of guys meeting Felix and Uly nearby to take the prisoners off our hands. When they get back, we roll." Everett was another one of Boone's guys. We hadn't seen him since Washington, D.C.

We waited a few minutes. Then Felix and Uly came back in the Range Rover. Eben retrieved Buddy from the bedroom. Eben, Malak, and Buddy got into the Range Rover and drove off. Ziv left the coach and followed the Range Rover in a cab. He refused to give up his role as the Monkey who watched the Leopard's tail.

We were headed for the Dogpatch.

MONDAY, SEPTEMBER 15 >

11:00 a.m. to 2:30 p.m. PST

Going to the Dogs

The first two locations we tried got us nothing. We drove to the next location in the Dogpatch and rolled to a stop in front of a run-down, junky-looking place. Cities tend to recycle their neighborhoods. In school we had learned about the history of the different sections of San Francisco such as the Marina District, the Presidio, and the Dogpatch. It was an old part of town that was full of abandoned warehouses and overgrown vacant lots. Parts of the Dogpatch were being rebuilt, some of the old buildings renovated and turned into apartments and condos. But there were still plenty of quiet, deserted, and out-of-the-way places.

Nobody knows for sure how it got the name Dogpatch. I remember learning that there used to be a kind of weed named "dog" something or other that grew there. Another legend said the name came from the packs of wild dogs that used to roam the area because it was close to the meatpacking district. Wild dogs. Packs of them. The way our luck had gone, that probably *was* how Dogpatch got its name. There were undoubtedly packs of wild dogs out there waiting for us right now. Then I thought that maybe Boone would know how the place got its name. He'd probably been to San Francisco since before there was a Dogpatch. Or even before there was a San Francisco. I hate how my mind races when I'm nervous.

As we climbed out of the coach, I looked around in every direction. The last thing I wanted was a bunch of wild dogs sneaking up on me.

"What are you doing?" Angela asked. Only she used that exasperated tone that older sisters sometimes get with younger brothers.

"Looking and listening for wild dogs," I said.

Angela sighed. "I'm not even going to ask."

X-Ray and Vanessa left the intellimobile and we all gathered in front of the building. It looked like it had been deserted for a very long time.

"Do you think Buddy is leading us on a wild goose chase? Is he taking us to a bunch of places to buy time for something? Maybe he and Number One have something planned?" Angela asked.

Boone shook his head. "I don't think so. Luckily for us, your mother sent Buddy's fear level off the charts. If he told another lie because he's trying to buy time or thinks he has some kind of escape plan or something . . . well, imagine what's running through ol' Buddy's mind right now. If I were to call your mom and say 'Buddy wasn't being truthful'? He might just die on the spot. Buddy is caught between a rock and a rock. He's afraid of this Number One, but he's also deathly afraid of the Leopard."

Boone turned to X-Ray. "I doubt there's any electronic surveillance around, but are you picking up anything?" It was the same question he'd asked X-Ray at the first two stops.

X-Ray was holding a tablet in his hand and he pressed the touchscreen a few times. "Nothing I wouldn't expect. Some cellular activity. But . . . I just enabled a scrambling protocol. If there are any cameras or audio devices nearby they just lost their signals. No one will know we're here."

The building had a big overhead garage door in the front. Next to it was an entry door. The entry door was locked, but X-Ray inserted a little device that looked like a souped-up, battery-operated screwdriver into the lock and the door popped open. Boone cautiously opened it. Inside there was a counter, with another door behind it.

"Croc," Boone said. Boone opened the door and Croc waddled through it. Inside he paused, sniffing the air, the floor, and worked his nose up and down the counter. He barked and Boone went in and opened the next door. Croc darted through it.

Croc had done the same thing at the first two buildings we searched. At the first one, I had wondered what he was doing. I was nervous and jerky, and for some reason, Boone sending Croc into the building before anyone else didn't exactly make me feel calm.

"What is he doing?" I'd whispered to Angela.

"Clearing the building and looking for booby traps would be my guess," she answered in a tone that implied I'd just asked the most obvious question in human history.

She was watching the door and didn't see me turn white.

Booby traps! I hadn't even considered that. Explosives! Guns! Knives held to my throat! Packs of wild dogs! Pigeon poop on my hands! And now I had to worry about booby traps? Maybe boarding school wouldn't be so bad after all.

Croc returned a few seconds later and woofed at Boone from the door.

"Let's go," he said.

We all entered the warehouse. It was a bigger building than it looked from the outside. At first there was nothing interesting or suspicious inside. A few wooden pallets and some broken crates were scattered about. But off in a far corner to the left sat a chair in front of some lights mounted on metal stands. They were the same kind of lights Mom and Roger used when they were on stage. I guessed we'd found the spot where Number One interrogated Buddy. In the movies and on TV you always see some poor sap getting a bright light shined in his eyes while the bad guy asks him questions from behind it.

Boone had us split up so we could cover more ground. I just didn't see anything that remotely resembled a clue. It was like all the other places we'd searched since this whole thing started.

Croc was over by the lights. He was sniffing a spot on the warehouse floor. And he was interested in something. He pawed at the ground, but I couldn't see anything from where I stood. Croc looked up at me and barked. Then he dug at the ground again.

I never know when it will happen or why it does. Maybe this time it was something in Croc's behavior that triggered it.

Because right then, I was hit full on with *the itch*. It's a feeling I get that something is wrong, or a major event is about to happen. Sometimes it's a good thing, like it warns me of trouble. It just hits me. My skin tingles, my nerves get all jangly, and the slightest noise can make me jump. It can be a bad thing, as in something dangerous, or it can be bad in the sense that I'm about to learn something I don't want to know. It's like a built-in warning system.

Crossing the warehouse floor toward Croc, I felt like I was walking through wet cement. My heart pumped so hard my blood made a roaring sound in my ears. Croc stared at me with his two different-colored eyes as I approached. It was disconcerting, as if he was trying really, really hard to tell me important information. When I finally reached him, he bent his head down and pushed something toward me with his muzzle.

It was a feather.

I picked it up off the floor. As soon as I touched it, *the itch* went through me like I'd been struck by lightning. The feather was brown and white and extremely rare. I knew this because I recognized it.

It belonged to my dad, the one, the only Speed Paulsen.

"Guys!" I yelled. "I got something."

Everyone hustled over to me and I handed the feather to Boone.

"What is it, Q?"

"It's a feather from the huia bird. They're from—were from—New Zealand. They're extinct now. I know this because Speed bought it at an auction. He loves feathers. Wears them in his clothing and costumes when he's on stage. Has them woven into his hair. He had it in one of his braids when he showed up in Virginia," I said.

Boone stared at the feather really hard. He wore a strange and curious expression on his face. Like he was trying to figure something out, or put several pieces of a puzzle together all at once.

"But your dad was going to the Florida Keys," Angela said. "How could he be here and how could he be Number One?"

"Because he's never been anything but a fake. A complete and total lying, deceiving fake," I said. "And think about it. He is . . . was . . . is a musician. He probably knows Buddy. I never knew my grandparents on my dad's side. They died when he was young, according to my mom. He was raised an orphan. Just like Buddy and a lot of the other members of the cell we've encountered. It fits," I said.

"It can't be," Angela said. "There has to be some other explanation."

"X-Ray," Boone said. He paused, staring at the feather like it was somehow the key to everything. "You remember that tracker I pulled from the coach back in Kitty Hawk? Does it still have a signal?"

X-Ray ran his fingertips over his tablet. "No. The battery is dead. But I can pull up the last known location," he said. A few more seconds passed as he tapped areas on the screen, muttering as he worked. "Its signal gets recorded . . . I can follow the movement and see the last–" X-Ray looked up at Boone. "It says it was in the Keys, Boone."

"But where in the Keys? Specifically. Find out the address

and what's there."

X-Ray slid his fingers back and forth. "Oh my," he said.

"What?" Boone asked.

"The address shows that the signal is coming from a Pak-n-Mail shipping store on Key West. And according to the log it was there since the day after you put it in his boot—until the unit quit transmitting about eighteen hours ago."

X-Ray frowned and looked at his tablet again. He gave it a slight shake, like he couldn't believe what it was telling him. It was the first time I'd ever seen him remotely question any piece of technology.

"He knew," Boone said. "Somehow he knew I put that tracker in his boot heel. He sent his boots to Key West because that's where he told us he was going."

"This can't be right, Boone," Vanessa said. "Speed? Speed Paulsen? That drug-addled moron is the leader of the ghost cell? I'm not buying it."

Boone was still staring at the feather. I'd never seen a look like this on his face. He was completely focused. On a feather.

"But, how, I mean . . ." Angela stammered. "I . . . Speed has a reputation as being . . ."

"An idiot?" I finished her sentence for her. "Because he's also a compulsive liar."

"I just don't see how . . ." X-Ray was as stunned as anyone else. He shook his tablet again, like maybe it was an Etch A Sketch and he could remake the whole last few minutes and somehow Speed wouldn't be Number One.

"It's him," Boone said. "It explains everything. Why he showed up in the middle of a hurricane in Virginia. Why Q was taken to Miss Ruby's ranch in San Antonio so he'd be out of the blast zone. He must have suspected Malak after Kitty Hawk so he took her off the board in Texas and sent her to Chicago. He's known Buddy for years. He's got money. He's traveled all over the world as a musician. It makes sense now."

"Not to me," Vanessa said, waving her hand in the air as if that settled it.

"I'm with Vanessa," X-Ray said. "No offense, Q, but I don't see how Speed is sm—able to carry this off. Not from what I know of him."

"But he did show up right in the middle of our . . ." Boone's words tailed off and he put his hand on his chin. It looked like he'd gained a few more gray hairs in the last couple of minutes.

My anger just kind of leaked out of me and I tried not to show anything, but I couldn't help it. My shoulders slumped, and I felt like I had no energy for any of this anymore. Croc sauntered over to me and pushed against my legs with his body. I reached down to pet him.

"Q? You okay?" Angela asked, quietly.

"No. No, Angela, I'm not okay at all. My dad lied to me again. He's been lying to me my whole life!" I kicked at the floor and stormed off away from the group. They stood there quietly, giving me space.

Finally, Angela walked over to me, followed by Croc.

"I'm sorry, Q. I really am. Is there anything I can do?"

Boone followed Angela and Croc, leaving X-Ray and Vanessa fidgeting by the light stands. "Q, there's something I need to tell you." He put one hand on my shoulder and handed me the feather. I wanted to wad it up and burn it.

"Listen to me," he said. "I know this just . . . well, it's horrible. But you did good work here. You figured it out. Now we know. We find Speed and we can stop this. I'm sorry, Q. I'm sorry Speed was—is—such a lousy excuse for a father. You're a great kid. You deserve better. Try to concentrate on the fact that you got a world-class mom. Right now you'd probably rather go off somewhere by yourself and just be alone. But you can't. I'm sorry. I need you to stick close. If he somehow finds out you're *not* with us, he might get suspicious and take off."

I looked up at Boone. "Are you saying my own dad had me kidnapped?" I was still thinking over what Boone said about me being taken to Miss Ruby's ranch in Texas.

"I am. I couldn't quite figure out why they would take you out of the blast zone in San Antonio. Just you and not Angela. Now I know."

I too had wondered why they separated us in San Antonio. Because he wanted to toy with us, showing us that he was some kind of criminal genius? He'd never displayed an ounce of interest in me in my entire life, unless there was a camera around. He wanted to save me in San Antonio, but was willing to let me die in a chemical attack in Chicago? My head was spinning. It was just too much. I mean, did his twisted mind think that this demonstrated he cared about me in some weird way? Did he think blowing up my mom, my friends and family, and a city full of innocent people, but not me, was "good parenting"? It all made me want to barf. I'd never understood his behavior. Now it made me even more confused. What kind of father does this?

"So now what do we do?" I asked.

"We find him," Boone said quietly.

"How? He's been miles ahead of us the whole way," I said.

Boone lowered his voice so only Angela and I could hear him. "I think I know how."

"Then tell me," I asked again. My head hurt. I couldn't imagine any way that Boone could find him.

"Because I think I might have an idea of what it is he's looking for," Boone said.

Getting Closer

Boone watched the dejection crawl across Q's face as the boy studied the feather in his hand. His heart broke for the kid. He knew in an instant what this was all about. What it had always been about.

Me. He thought. *It's about me. It's about the power. The blink.*

He'd had many names in the more than nine hundred years he'd been alive. Tyrone Boone was just the latest. He'd used it for a while now. With any luck, he'd never have to change his name or identity again.

He'd spent hundreds of years asking himself the same set of questions.

Why me?

Why was I chosen?

How have I lived so long?

How can I finish this?

Now it seemed he was closer to the answers than he had ever been.

He would have spared Q and Angela all of this had he

been able to. What amazing kids they were. He would have given anything to spare Q the heartbreak he was feeling. Or to give Angela back all those years with her mother that she had lost.

I'm going to have to tell them the truth. Soon.

It was something he'd never told anyone. Not once in nearly a millennia. But he could not finish this without their help. And for that they deserved the truth.

A part of him wondered if he could stop it. Speed was younger. Boone was old. He was slowing down. It was taking him days to regenerate when, many years ago, it had taken a few hours at most.

Q and Angela stood there looking at him. Waiting for him to say something. To issue an order or a command that would set them on the path of putting an end to this.

"Okay, let's get back on the coach," Boone said to everyone. "But for now, the fact that we know Speed is Number One stays between us. We're not even going to tell the rest of the group yet. We want Buddy to think he still has an ace in the hole. Besides, if he finds out we know, he might try harder to give us the slip. Vanessa and X-Ray, you leave in the intellimobile and hook up with Malak and Eben and the rest. Find that box. Q and Angela, I'll be out in a minute. Croc and I are going to take one last look around, make sure there isn't anything else here we can use."

Q handed the feather back to Boone and they all filed out.

When they were gone he spun the feather in his fingers as he studied it. Croc huffed at him.

"I know. It's been so long, old friend. But it looks like

we've finally found him. We can end this." Croc huffed and scratched at Boone's leg, then sat back on his haunches. He looked at Boone and cocked his head.

"No, I haven't forgotten," Boone said. "You're right. I'm not fully recovered. But he's been blinking all over the place, just like we have. He's got to be as run-down as we are. Right now his name is 'Slow Paulsen.' Don't worry. When he makes his move, we'll be ready."

Croc huffed again.

"Stop being so negative," Boone said to him. "We've never been this close. He has it. I'm positive it's what he has Buddy looking for. I'll bet you an order of kung pao chicken. We can get it back. Then it will all be over."

Croc stood up from sitting on his haunches as if he'd made his point and had nothing else to say. He strolled past Boone and headed toward the door and the waiting coach.

"Everybody's a critic," Boone muttered as he sauntered along behind him. "Then why don't you come up with a better plan?" he said, but Croc ignored him. As Boone and Croc exited the building, Boone looked up at the sun and took a long, deep breath of fresh air. He smiled.

Life, even one as long as mine, is all about being grateful for the little things.

The Little Things

Vanessa and X-Ray had returned to the intellimobile and driven off as Boone instructed. Angela sat at the dining table looking at something on her laptop.

"Where's Q?" Boone asked.

"He said he didn't feel well. He's lying down in the bedroom," she said.

Boone looked back at the bedroom door. Croc hopped up in the shotgun seat and curled up in a ball.

"What is the plan now?" Angela asked.

"We're not going to lose, Angela—don't worry," Boone said. "In fact it's time to turn up the heat on Buddy T."

Boone punched a button on his phone.

"Felix, put Buddy on," he said. He put the phone on speaker.

"What is it, Boone?" Buddy said, sounding annoyed.

"You're holding out on me, Buddy." Angela looked up from her computer and leaned in closer to the phone.

"What? What are you talking about? I told you where—"

"You told me nothing," Boone interrupted. "There's nothing here, Buddy. You lied. I don't cotton to being lied to. Where's the box?"

"I don't know, Boone. I *told* you there wouldn't be anything there. You don't understand this guy. He's freaky. It's not my fault you didn't find any leads. I swear. I can't remember where this thing is and–" Buddy was pleading, when Boone interrupted.

"Okay, Buddy. Play it your way. I think you're stalling and stringing us along. You're hoping Number One finds out we got our hooks in you and he just disappears. It's how you ghost cell types do it, right? You just fade away. I think your whole story is a lie. Once you're convinced Number One is gone, you've got some elaborate scheme in place to ditch us. So I'm sorry to inform you, Buddy T., but your little charade is over. I'm going to cut you loose."

"You what? No! You can't do that! If he knows . . . we had an agreement . . . he'll kill me. You don't know who you're dealing with. This guy . . . there's something different about him. It's like he's everywhere at once . . . he knows things . . . things he couldn't know unless he'd seen them himself, but he couldn't have seen them because he was never there. I know how crazy it sounds, Boone! Please, you can't do this!"

Boone tried not to smile. Buddy's description was what he'd been waiting for. Now he was more convinced than ever that he was right about Speed.

Boone was silent for several moments, letting Buddy sweat a little.

"Okay, Buddy. Then I suggest you think real hard about

finding that box. Where is it?"

"I don't . . . look . . . he told me how big it was. There's about three banks left where I rented big boxes. It must . . . maybe it's in one of them. But, Boone, he's given me so much stuff. Old stuff. I don't mean just antiques, I mean really old stuff that would be hard to get. It has to be in one of those. I'll try to find it and—"

"You better find it. Or you can take your chances with Number One," Boone said. "Put Felix back on the line."

"Yeah, Boone," Felix said.

"Where are you?"

"We just checked State Federal downtown. Nothing."

"Okay, Buddy says he's got some locations with extra-large boxes. Head there next. I'm sending X-Ray and Vanessa to you. They'll take Buddy, Malak, and Eben in the intellimobile. You, Uly, and Pat take the Rover. Then wait for my call. I want to make sure Q and Angela are someplace safe until we find what Number One is looking for. I'll call you with the location, and then I want you guys to run countersurveillance on us."

"Copy that," Felix said and disconnected the call.

"What is going on, Boone?" Angela asked.

"I don't know for sure. But I think we're close. But we've got to find that box. Come on, I need to talk to Q."

Angela stood up and followed Boone as he headed for the back of the coach.

Handling the Truth

I heard the knock on the bedroom door. My hands had worked through my deck of cards what felt like a thousand times since I lay down on the bed. Now I was practicing with my magic coin. I didn't want to talk to anyone. More knocking.

"Q?" Boone said through the door. "Is it okay if Angela and I come in?"

I didn't answer. Having a dad like Speed Paulsen is bad enough all by itself. There's the lies, the forgotten birthdays, the fights between him and my mom. Now it turns out he's also the world's biggest and baddest terrorist. I just couldn't imagine how my life could get any worse.

"Q? Can we please come in?" Boone asked again.

"Fine," I said.

They opened the door and strode in. I didn't get up off the bed.

"I'm changing things up. Buddy is feeling even more pressure now. And since we know that Speed is Number One, I want to get you and Angela someplace a little off the grid.

Not the hotel. Someplace he wouldn't think to look. Do you have any ideas?"

I was quiet for a moment, rolling my magic coin back and forth through my fingers. The truth of it was, I was just tired. Finding out about Speed made it feel like the whole world was just pressing down on me. Boone seemed to sense how I was feeling. Angela just stood there biting her lower lip.

"Q, I know this—"

"Please, Boone. Stop. I just don't want to think about it right now."

"I understand. But I've got to move you someplace safe and—"

I held up my hand to stop him, pulled out my recently cloned phone, and called Mom.

"Q?" she said. I could tell by her voice she was still a little angry with me.

"Hi, Mom. How you doing?" I said.

"I'm okay. What's up?"

"First, I wanted to say I'm sorry about what happened at the airport. I don't know what got into me. I guess . . . I don't know. Anyway, I just had a question. I know we sold the sailboat to the Hackworths before we left on the tour. But Boone is here with Angela and me now, and I was just telling them about how cool it was when we lived on it. I know they're out of town a lot. Do you think you could call them and ask if I could show Boone and Angela the boat? Just for a while. I'd like to see it again before . . . you know. Boarding school."

A little extra guilt couldn't hurt.

Mom was quiet a moment. I could tell she was trying to

determine if I was up to something. But eventually she gave in. "You know what? I think that's a *great* idea. I'll get in touch with Mrs. Hackworth and ask if it's okay if you come by. Let me call you right back." She disconnected.

I didn't move from the phone, still maneuvering the coin through my fingers.

Boone and Angela didn't say anything. They just shifted their weight from foot to foot and looked uncomfortable. I didn't like that they were upset and worried about me. It wasn't their fault.

"You guys want to see a cool card trick?" I said.

"Uh. Sure," Angela said. But my phone rang before I could retrieve one of my decks.

"Hi, Mom."

"Hi, kiddo. I have good news. I just talked to Mrs. Hackworth and they are out of town this week. She said you could spend as much time on the boat as you want. There is a spare set of keys at the marina office. Is everything else okay? Where are you?"

"Everything is fine, Mom. We're in the coach with Boone, getting some of our clothes and stuff before we check into the hotel. See you at the concert, all right?"

"You bet, sweetie. Have fun."

"We will. Thanks, Mom. I love you," I said.

"Love you too, babe. Bye." She disconnected.

I looked at Boone. "We can go to the boat. It's probably the last place Speed would think to look."

"Okay, that's perfect," Boone said. "We'll get–"

"On one condition," I interrupted.

Boone stopped and stared at me, a wary look in his eye.

"Once we get there, you tell us everything. And I mean *everything*."

Boone considered this for a moment.

"Deal," he said.

Good Knight

The three of us hopped a cab to the marina. We left the coach parked where it was. It wouldn't do any good to have the huge Match coach in the marina parking lot. Not when we were trying to stay off the radar. The keys to the sailboat were waiting in the marina office, as promised. Uly, Felix, and Pat had cleared the marina and reported back to Boone that it was safe. No one was watching the boat. Pat, Felix, and Uly were now running countersurveillance on the moorage. The Range Rover was out of sight.

The sun was bright and Angela, Boone, and I sat on the deck of the sailboat. I was surprised by how much I'd missed it. Ever since Mom and Roger started the tour, it felt like I'd been riding a whirlwind. Being in a peaceful, familiar setting had a calming effect on all of us. If it's even possible to be calm after determining your father is secretly the world's most wanted terrorist.

There was a small quarterdeck at the stern, holding a table surrounded by cushioned benches. Angela opened her backpack and removed her laptop and file folder full of papers. She laid the file on the table in front of Boone. Inside it were copies of all the pictures P.K. had sent us, plus more info we'd dug up on our own.

Boone took a few moments to look through the file. When he was finished, he handed it back to Angela.

"I assume this is mostly your work?" Boone said to her.

"Mostly. Q helped, and we got some of it from P.K.," she said.

Boone sighed. "P.K. I should have known. I'll bet he went to the National Archives, didn't he?" He held up the folder. "Angela, you're going to make one heck of an agent someday," he said.

"Who are you, Boone?" she asked.

"What are you, Boone?" I asked.

"I'm just a man. An exhausted old man," he said.

"I think you're more than that," Angela said.

"I suppose that's true," Boone said.

"Boone, I don't want to be a hard case," I said. "But this is the first chance we've had to be alone for an extended period of time since Kitty Hawk. You've been intentionally dodging us ever since then. We know what you can do. I think we've earned an explanation."

"It's complicated," Boone said.

"Most things are," Angela shot back.

Boone sighed deeply and leaned back on the bench.

"No, Angela," Boone said. "Truthfully, they're not. Most things are pretty simple. Right versus wrong. Good versus evil. Morality versus immorality. You can argue the details, but the

big things? They're not so hard to figure out. It's people who
screw them up."

Angela and I didn't say anything. We were content to wait
until Boone was ready to tell us.

"My real name is Sir Tonye Borneo. The photo you found
of the statue? It comes from my family estate. I was born in
the year 1080. When I was twenty, I was knighted and in
1104 I was sent with eight other knights to Jerusalem. We had
offered our swords and shields to the pope. He sent us there
with the assigned duty of protecting Christian pilgrims on the
roads to and from the holy city. Jerusalem was then under the
stewardship of King Baldwin II. Grateful for our service, he
gave us horses and weaponry and allowed us to establish our
barracks in Solomon's Temple."

"The Knights Templar," Angela said quietly. "Oh, my
God. You were a Templar knight? I can't . . . seriously?" All of
a sudden she sat up in her seat and her eyes were wide. The
palms of her hands were pressed down on the table, like she
couldn't believe what she was hearing.

I just sat there. I had no idea what they were talking
about. Something about some knights who lived in a temple.
Apparently this was a big deal.

Boone nodded. "Yes. Officially we were known as the
Poor Fellow-Soldiers of Christ and King Solomon's Temple,
but that's a mouthful. Eventually, we were simply referred to
as the Knights Templar, or Templars."

"Wow," Angela said. "I–I just . . . wow!"

"So you were, like, knights in armor, running around
fighting and stuff?" I asked.

Boone chuckled. He seemed more relaxed than at any time since I'd stumbled across him in the desert. Maybe unburdening himself was giving his spirits a lift.

"No, not armor like you see in the movies where knights are jousting on horseback. That wasn't invented until much later. We had iron helmets and shin guards, but we mostly wore chain mail. Astride a horse, small iron lances were our weapons of choice, but we also fought with sword and shield. We trained to fight nonstop. You have to understand, back then, a single well-mounted, well-armed knight could strike fear in a half-dozen bandits or raiders who might be harassing innocents."

"So you were actually there when the Knights Templar were founded?" Angela said. She still seemed a little freaked out by Boone's revelation.

"Yes," Boone said. "And as it turns out, I'm still here. I never thought I'd be here so long."

"So you're not some kind of wizard, or the world's greatest magician or a time traveler or something, are you? Because if you're the world's greatest magician I'm going to be really ticked," I said. "You know that's always been my goal."

Boone laughed. "No, Q, I'm not a wizard or magician or any of those things. I'm not even immortal. At least I believe I can be killed. Or at least eventually I'll get to the point that I can be killed. I think. I'm not exactly sure. In fact, it's almost happened on more than one occasion. I've been shot at at least sixteen times, stabbed more times than I can count. But I always recover. I still heal because of what happened. Though lately it seems to take a lot longer than it used to."

"Are you saying you have some kind of magical healing power?" Angela asked.

"Yes. That's what I'm saying."

"So you can heal yourself *and* poof all over the place as well?" I groaned. My plans for learning the secret of Boone's ability seemed further and further away.

"Poof?" Boone asked.

"When you disappear and reappear. I call it poofing," I explained.

"Poof. Huh. I guess that's as good a word as any," Boone said. Croc was curled up at his feet, and he reached down and patted the dog on the head. "Croc and I call it 'blinking.' Because that's what it seems like to us. We go from point A to point B in the blink of an eye." As if to emphasize the idea, Croc lifted his head, opened his blue eye, and then shut it again.

"But how, Boone?" Angela asked. "How do you do it? Were you born this way? Is it some kind of occult thing? Did you discover the secret to faster-than-light travel?"

"No. Nothing like that. It goes back to Jerusalem. Remember when I told you how King Baldwin let us billet in King Solomon's Temple?"

"Yes?" Angela and I said at the same time.

"It all started . . . everything began when we found something there," Boone said. "Something very powerful."

Angela reached into her backpack and pulled out a small digital recorder. She put it on the table. "Boone. If it's okay, I think we should record you. Just in case something . . . happens to you . . . we might need to know everything you've told us. If we get something wrong–"

"I think that's a good idea," Boone said. He took a deep breath and looked out at the sparkling blue water. He began speaking and his voice took on a tone I'd never heard him use before. No good ol' boy twang. No regular, gruff Boone voice like he used when he was issuing orders to Felix, Uly, or X-Ray. It was serious and formal. There was an intensity in his words I'd never heard despite all we'd been through in the last few days.

"I should probably start at the beginning," Boone said.

And he did.

CE 1104–1106 ❯

Boone

I was my father's second son.

In the Middle Ages the second son was unlucky in birth, having far fewer options than the firstborn. My father was a nobleman in southern Italy. My older brother became a priest. Like many younger brothers in the noble classes, that placed certain limitations on my future occupations. My father owned one of the largest estates in all of southern Italy. In those days the oldest brother went to the priesthood—the real power resided with the church—and the younger brothers could either manage their father's lands, waiting for their fathers to die, so they could become barons themselves, or they could train to become knights.

We lived in an incredibly violent time. Europe was just starting to emerge from the Dark Ages. For years, the kingdoms in England, Ireland, France, and the rest of the European continent had been in a state of near-constant warfare. If they weren't fighting Viking raiders from the north they were fighting each other. And when the Vikings were finally beaten back, the kingdoms turned on each other. Fighting men were always in short supply, and that was the path I chose. Fighting.

I had no interest in farming or vineyards or being a baron. Knighthood was far more exciting. From the age of fourteen, I trained in the arts of war. Horseback riding, archery, sword fighting, and the use of the cavalry lance occupied my days from dawn to dusk. My father hired the best instructors to teach me. I spent hours in the saddle.

Sword fighting was the same. I'll never forget my first lesson. I had a helmet but nothing else for protection. One of my father's men-at-arms had been tasked with teaching me. We used wooden swords and he beat me nearly senseless.

"Are you ready, young Borneo?" he asked me.

"Yes," I answered, holding my sword by the hilt, squeezing it as hard as I could.

"Good," he said. And then he proceeded to hammer me into the ground. His first blow struck me above the wrist. The pain caused me to lose feeling in my arm. I dropped the sword. Next came a blow to the side of my head and I fell face first into the dirt.

"Were these real swords, you would have lost an arm and your head, in that order," he said. "Get up. Again."

I crawled to my feet and the same scenario repeated itself. I've been in hundreds of battles and fights in my life, but I don't know if I've ever been more tired and sore than I was at the end of that first day. Fencing is a sport. Sword fighting is combat.

I didn't just train with the sword. I became familiar in the use of all of the weapons of the time, although I'll admit I was never much of an archer. Oh, I could hit what I aimed at. But it always seemed to require more patience and skill than I possessed. Nevertheless, as the years passed and as I grew to adulthood I became—let's just call me fierce.

By the time I was twenty I was a fighting machine. A soldier. But a soldier needs a war. A place where all the skills and training and hours of practice can be put to use.

An enemy.

In 1104 I found them all.

My father was friendly with a knight from a neighboring barony. His name was Hughes de Payans. One morning he rode up to our estate, asking for an audience with my father. And he asked that I be included in the conversation.

We sat in my father's council hall, the place where he did his official business. Hughes was tall and rugged. Strong and well trained.

"I come with news from Rome," he said. "I have been in conference with the pope."

My father was a quiet man, not prone to talk. But he was astute.

"And what does His Holiness require of us now?" he asked cautiously. My father and Hughes were friendly, but an official envoy from the pope was something to be handled delicately.

"There is trouble in Jerusalem," Hughes said.

"Isn't there always trouble in Jerusalem?" my father asked.

Hughes chuckled and I saw my father visibly relax. My father was good at reading people. It's something I inherited from him. Hughes's laughter told him the visit was a courtesy.

"His Holiness has tasked me to raise a group of knights.

With them we will travel to the Holy Land and offer our swords to King Baldwin, ruler of Jerusalem. Word has reached Rome that bandits and the local tribes are harassing Christian pilgrims. We will offer them protection."

"And what does this have to do with us?" my father asked.

"Word of your son's training has reached me. I understand he has become quite formidable."

"He is also quite young," my father answered sharply.

"Father– " I interrupted. He held up his hand. I understood. Sir Hughes wanted me to fight with him!

"No doubt. And we will need his youth and his vigor. I've heard talk, Baron Borneo. Your son is an excellent rider. Some say he is second to none with the long sword." He paused and looked at me. "That I will need to see for myself."

My father was quiet as he considered Sir Hughes's request. I could tell he was about to say no, and apparently so could Hughes.

"My Lord Borneo," he said. "I understand. You have two sons. One becomes a priest. You wonder and worry who will take care of your lands–"

"I care nothing of my *lands*," my father snapped. "I care very much for my *sons*."

"I did not come to anger you," Hughes said. "We have been friends. We have fought together ourselves. You–"

"And we have watched men die. My son has not. I would spare him of it," my father interrupted.

Sir Hughes closed his eyes and nodded. "Indeed we have," he said. "And I would spare him of it as well, were I you. But the word has been given and it must be answered. And forgive me, my friend. I came to you, first, as a courtesy. But is your son not of age? Should it not be his decision?"

I *was* of age. Had I not been so absorbed in training, I would have–should have–taken a wife and been raising a family by then. But I wanted to fight.

"He is," my father said quietly. "How much time does he have?" My father asked Sir Hughes because he already knew my answer.

I would go to the Holy Land. I would fight.

It was the worst decision I ever made in my life.

The Holy Land

Three days later I said good-bye to my father.

"Father . . . I promise, I will return home. I will remember everything you have taught me."

"Do not make promises you cannot keep," he said. "Be safe. Pay attention. Follow Sir Hughes's instructions without fail, for your life depends on it. You might come home alive."

As parting words, those may sound harsh. But it was my father's way of telling me he loved me. I know that now. A year after I left, he fell ill with a fever and died. That was the last day I saw him.

With Croc at my side, I rode to Sir Hughes's estate and we departed for the Holy Land a few days later. I could barely contain my excitement. The ship traveled slowly. Impossibly slowly, it seemed to me. Back then, sailing ships were simple, single-mast vessels with a square canvas sail. When there was no wind they were rowed by oarsmen. Today, a trip that takes two days by sea took over two weeks nine hundred years ago. I was itching for a fight.

I found it quickly.

We arrived in the city of Acre, which is on the northern coast of what now is Israel. We gave the horses a few days' time to rest and recover from their voyage. We hired porters to assist our squires with our equipment, mounted up, and headed out for Jerusalem.

It was my first lesson in learning that spies are everywhere.

In a hotbed of such violence, anger, and religious fervor, spies were more numerous than the olives on the olive trees that dotted the countryside. Or so it seemed. It was a perilous introduction to the hazards and advantages of covert intelligence. I learned a hard lesson: that there is nothing more valuable than knowing something about your enemy and them not knowing that you know. Does that make sense? There is no replacement for a highly trained operative. All the technology we have today? None of it can take the place of a human being. Those things have their place, of course. But a well-placed spy, an agent behind enemy lines, someone who wins the confidence and learns, sees, and hears the secrets of your enemy? There is no piece of technology better than that.

One of the porters we hired to help carry our equipment was in the employ of a local tribal chieftain who thought slaughtering nine knights sent by the pope would bring great glory upon him. We were attacked the very first night on the trail.

After making camp, we posted sentries. One of those sentries was the spy, who let the chieftain's men inside the camp. First they slew the porters, whom they considered traitors for agreeing to work for us. Then they came after us.

"To arms! To arms!" The shouting woke me and my sword was instantly in my hand. The moon and firelight gave us enough light to see. I leaped to my feet, just in time to parry the downward swing of an angry man with a long and deadly scimitar. We struggled hand to hand, grappling and punching, gouging at each other's eyes. He bit me on the shoulder, but I held firm. He did not. I had a dagger at my belt and with my free hand, I used it.

Someone somewhere in the darkness yelled, "Be glorious!"

For whatever reason, it invigorated us. We all began to shout it as we fought. Even the squires, who were also trained in combat, acquitted themselves well that night. "Be glorious! Be glorious!" We chanted over and over, louder each time.

The chieftain and his men found our behavior unnerving.

Attacking poorly armed or defenseless pilgrims was one thing, but it was soon apparent they had never encountered well-trained, well-equipped knights. Even betrayed and taken by surprise, we fought like demons. Two of our squires were injured, but the nine of us either killed or wounded thirty men. It was the beginning of the building of our carefully crafted reputation as ferocious fighters. Even Croc got in on the action, leaping high to knock one of the raiders from the saddle. After that night he became the official mascot of our group.

News of our victory traveled quickly and we made it safely to Jerusalem, though enemy forces shadowed us the entire time. King Baldwin treated us like heroes. Our enemies constantly besieged the city and we plunged into the fighting almost the very next day. The king was so grateful he gave us shelter in Solomon's Temple. We pledged our swords and lives to the king and our cause. Sir Hughes declared that we would be known as the Poor Fellow-Soldiers of Christ and King Solomon's Temple. Eventually, because we lived in the temple, the locals began referring to us as the Knights Templar. The name stuck.

Sir Hughes began developing our fighting strategies after our first few skirmishes. "We will work in groups of three, patrolling all roads leading in and out of the city. We ride on our warhorses and escort any pilgrims we find to safety. In everything we do, we show confidence, aggression, and an utter lack of fear. No. Fear. We will carry our banner high at all times. And we will wear these."

He handed us each a white tunic with a brilliant red cross emblazoned across the chest. These fit perfectly over our chain mail. And in the desert they were visible from miles away. We wore them every day as we chased down bandits and raiders and protected all who traveled the roads. Word of our exploits spread throughout the region. The attacks on innocent victims diminished. And the story could have ended there. Nine brave men who fought for a cause they believed in.

And it might have–if Sir Hughes and I hadn't made a remarkable discovery in King Solomon's Temple.

The Discovery

It wasn't the original Temple of King Solomon. The first temple was destroyed and the one where we stayed had been rebuilt over the original site, or so it was said, but no one was certain. Remember, this was one thousand years ago. There were no real records, no maps or photographs. Just oral tradition and legend and half-truths.

Sir Hughes became obsessed with the temple. He would pace off the rooms. He spent hours measuring walls and making sketches, and inspecting the building from top to bottom. None of the other knights paid much attention, but he had assigned me to his squad—I believe he felt he owed it to my father to watch over me—so I was usually sleeping while he spent his off hours examining every inch of one of the most holy places in the city.

One night, Sir Hughes placed his gloved hand over my mouth and roused me from my sleep. I shared sleeping quarters with Quintas, a brother knight, who snored softly on the pallet across the room from me. He was a heavy sleeper, and it was unlikely he would awaken. Croc woke up and growled in curiosity. Sir Hughes shushed him.

"Do not make a sound," Sir Hughes whispered. "Follow me."

Out of habit, I grabbed my sword. In my half-awake state I wondered if I was needed for battle or if we were under attack. Sir Hughes laughed when he noticed my sword gleaming in the flickering torchlight that lined the temple walls. Croc padded along at my side, his ears up, just as curious as I was.

"No, young Borneo," he chuckled. "Sheath your blade. We have nothing to fear this night."

He led me to a wall along the southern end of the temple. We stood before it and he placed his hands on the bricks as if he were praying. I was confused and tired. I'd spent many hours in the saddle that day. Why he had summoned me here escaped me.

"Um. Sir Hughes," I said. "May I ask what we are doing here in the middle of the night?"

"What do you know of this temple?" he asked.

"Only that it is a replacement for the original."

"Did you know that it was once thought to house the holiest of relics? The Ark of the Covenant, the One True Cross, some say even the Holy Grail itself was kept here."

"But surely that must be . . . it can't . . . Sir Hughes, why would such valuable items be kept here?"

"No one knows for sure, of course. The first temple was destroyed during the siege of Jerusalem in the sixth century. King David attempted to rebuild it, but its construction eventually fell to his son Solomon."

"Sir Hughes, I have observed your . . . behavior. What

interests you so about this place?"

"If the holy relics were here, suppose they survived the destruction of the first temple. Where did they go? Do you not think someone would have made sure they were safe? And returned them here, where they could be further safeguarded?"

"Yes. I suppose, but . . ." I could not understand his obsession. Even if the relics were here once, it was doubtful they still were. They could be anywhere.

"You think I'm crazy!"

"No! Of course not!"

Sir Hughes laughed. "Do not fear, young Borneo. I do not fault your skepticism. Except your information is incomplete."

"Sir?"

"When I visited your father's estate, I had just returned from the Vatican. There the pope himself showed me proof–a batch of letters written by priests who secreted the relics out of the city when it was besieged and the Temple destroyed. For years they kept them safe, always on the move, often hidden in nothing more than primitive caves. As the years passed, the priests recruited new members to their group to keep the relics safe. Their goal was to rebuild the Temple and return the artifacts to safety. And it would appear from the letters they were successful."

"But where?" I did not say it, but it seemed to me that Sir Hughes was placing a great amount of faith in some old letters written by a group of questionable guardians.

"Right here," he said, patting the bricks. "Behind this wall."

Digging

Sir Hughes and I went to work on the bricks with our daggers, carefully chipping away at the mortar between them. For hours that night we worked in the glowing torchlight. You must understand. It's different now. We put all of our most valuable things—works of art, antiques, documents like the Constitution and the Declaration of Independence—in museums and carefully built archives.

In those days, nothing like that existed. There were paintings and statues adorning buildings. The temple itself was decorated with tapestries and other works of art. But to find the Ark of the Covenant? The One True Cross? The Holy Grail? To discover that the most sacred relics in all of Christendom not only existed, but to set eyes on them? The possibility was too exciting.

"My measuring and pacing, which looked so strange to you, led me here," Sir Hughes said as we worked. "I discovered that this interior wall stops nearly twenty paces short of the exterior wall. There is no door or entrance. I believe it encloses a hidden room. Someone went to a great deal of trouble to conceal it. And why would they do that if not to hide something valuable? It does not conceal a column or support the weight of the roof. I can find no other architectural reason for this space to exist. It must be here for some other purpose. What if it is true, young Borneo? What if we are about to make the greatest discovery yet made by mortal men?"

His excitement was infectious. Croc seemed to sense my exhilaration and as we worked, he paced about, keeping watch and sniffing the air, ready to warn us should anyone approach. Sir Hughes told me more of what he learned by poring over documents in Rome. After a while, his story started to sound plausible. He had found multiple sources, different texts and scrolls that pointed toward a small group of men who had spirited the relics away hundreds of years ago and then secretly restored them to the Temple when it was rebuilt.

It had been much harder and more tedious work to remove the bricks than it would have been to knock the wall down. But as Sir Hughes explained, the Temple was one of the holiest places in Jerusalem. What we were doing, if we were wrong, bordered on desecration. Still, as we stood there soaked in sweat from work and anticipation, we cast our torches about, expecting to find a vast store of relics.

We finally removed enough bricks to see that there was indeed a void space behind the wall. It was a hidden room. If Sir Hughes's information was correct it should be full of relics.

There was nothing there.

At first the disappointment was overwhelming. The

room was nearly empty. A few bricks and tattered, rolled parchments were scattered about the floor. The space held no ornate cabinets that might house the One True Cross. Nor was there any sight of the Ark of the Covenant, which legend said housed the actual stone tablets upon which Moses had inscribed the Ten Commandments. Only dust and spiderwebs and our frustration occupied the room.

The flickering torchlight revealed the despair etched on Sir Hughes's face. I understood then. He had not come to the Holy Land just to protect pilgrims. He had come for this. Fighting and defending the weak and innocent may have been his primary mission. But finding these relics was what drove him. To recover and protect them and carry on the work of the priests who had safeguarded them was his true calling. Perhaps he had even been ordered to do so by the pope himself.

We stood silent for several minutes. Sir Hughes took his torch to every corner of the room, looking for any sign that he might have been right. But it appeared as if this space had not been disturbed for dozens, if not hundreds, of years.

At first it was barely noticeable. But from someplace, either within the room or nearby, came a faint, barely audible humming. In a few seconds the noise was all around us. Croc became agitated, his superior hearing picking up the noise loud and clear.

"I assume you hear that?" Sir Hughes asked.

"Yes . . . but where is it?" I turned about, looking for the source of the strange sound.

Croc padded across the room, his paws kicking up dust.

He jumped and clawed at a spot on the wall, barking and growling.

"You must keep him silent," Sir Hughes hissed. "No one can discover us here!"

"Croc, off. To me," I said. But it was one of the rare times Croc has ever disobeyed me. He was obsessed with something in that spot. He scratched and dug at the wall.

Then a strange glow came from a small crack in the place where he was digging. It was a faint blue, but as we drew closer to it, the color deepened. A small alcove was carved in the wall and covered with a lead panel. Either Croc had knocked it loose, or over time the panel had shifted and now the light escaped through the tiny opening. Using his dagger, Hughes pried the panel off—and there it was.

It was a cup sitting on a pedestal, and the light was coming *from* it. Almost as if it contained its own power source or as if a fire of some kind burned within it. It grew so bright we had to shield our eyes. Then the color faded and we were left with only the torchlight again.

"What just happened?" I asked. "What is this?"

"I do not know for certain, young Borneo," Sir Hughes said. "But I have an idea."

In those brief seconds my life changed forever. And it is why I sit here before you. It is why I am able to do what I do—what you call the *poof!* And it is why I've lived nearly a thousand years. More than that, I believe it is the power behind the ghost cell.

And we must find it or–through no fault of its own–it will destroy us all.

The Stuff of Legend

It was the Holy Grail.

Sir Hughes had been right. The other relics had been removed, perhaps looted or deemed too valuable to all be kept in one location. But the Grail had remained hidden in its safe spot. The light had glowed brightly for perhaps a minute. Then it dimmed, until it disappeared.

"Did you see that? What just happened?" I asked Sir Hughes, consumed with questions. My heart raced.

I know it sounds ridiculous to you now. Why would a briefly glowing light stir such a feeling in us? Again, remember this was the twelfth century. To us, what we had just seen had sparked our curiosity, mixed with a healthy dose of fear. Imagine how you might feel if a flying saucer were to suddenly appear over your head–something you clearly knew was otherworldly or outside the realm of our current level of technology and intellectual understanding. Then you might have a glimpse into our mindset at the time.

"I do not know," Sir Hughes said. "We . . . I . . . need

time to consider this." He examined the small alcove and the panel that had concealed it. "How strange they would use lead to cover it, since there are so many other, stronger materials to keep it safe," he muttered. "Perhaps the lead shields it in some way, keeps the light from leaking out." He continued his examination, calmly and without haste, muttering as he looked at the cup.

"Sir Hughes, do you think . . . is it true? Could this be—" But I couldn't say the words. Legends of the cup of Christ were too numerous to mention. But until that moment, I believed that was all they were. Legends.

Hughes gently placed the cup back in the small alcove and replaced the lead panel covering it.

"Come, young Borneo," he said. "We must return to our barracks and sleep on this. Perhaps the hand of God will guide us. Until then, mention this to no one, not even Quintas."

"As you command, Sir Hughes," I said.

When I turned toward the opening we had made in the wall, I was suddenly *across the room* in a heartbeat. I had been standing next to Sir Hughes at the alcove and the next instant I was at the opening itself. Much like what happened to you in Chicago, Q, I felt a wave of nausea wash over me. I vomited on the spot. My head spun and I sank to the ground. Sir Hughes rushed to my side.

"Tonye," he said, and he almost never called me that. Always it was "young Borneo" or "Sir Borneo."

"What happened? Are you ill? How did you do that?" He peppered me with questions I could not answer. I was too dizzy.

"I . . . I . . . do not know," I said to him. And I didn't. It just happened. I had been given a command, and without thinking I followed the order. Now I felt disoriented and sick.

Sir Hughes helped me through the opening. I had to wait, slumped against the wall while he worked as quickly as he could, carefully replacing the bricks we had removed.

"Are you able to walk?" he asked.

"I think so." I was weak and shaking. Wondering if I would suddenly "jump" like I had in the chamber. Taking one last look at the wall, he took me by the arm and led me back to our sleeping quarters.

"Again, young Borneo," he cautioned, his voice low, "you can tell *no one* of what we have found. And especially what happened to you. Any word of this would see us both hanged as heretics."

I staggered to my bunk. Croc curled up at my feet. Quintas still snored away. I doubted he had stirred since I'd left a few hours earlier. I was exhausted. However, I could not sleep. By turns I was fascinated and frightened by what had happened to me. Part of me was afraid to close my eyes–worried I might wake up across the room. Or somewhere else that might require an explanation I was not prepared to give.

There was no sleeping for me that night; I tossed and turned until dawn. At first light we roused ourselves to ride out on patrol. Sir Hughes met Quintas and me at the stables. He made no mention of the night's events. The three of us were silent as we rode out onto the main road leading west from Jerusalem. As he always did, Croc raced ahead of us, back and forth, acting as an early-warning system.

Sir Hughes was one of the best military commanders I've known. We were a small unit, surrounded by a superior force composed of enemies who had hated us for centuries. But Sir Hughes understood the psychological aspects of warfare.

We rode in bright white tunics with red crosses emblazoned across our chests. You could almost say they were targets. But we did not sit back and act like targets. We attacked. The bandits and tribesmen we battled were disorganized but dangerous. Sir Hughes's tactics confounded them. Our mail, helmets, and weapons were always polished to a high sheen. Our horses were resplendent, giant destriers that also wore armor and bright white coverlets to protect them from the sun. Our appearance was a statement. Whenever we rode out of the city, Sir Hughes would repeat in Latin, *Ecce ferox, saevire* over and over. Loosely translated, it means "Look fierce, be fierce." And so we did.

"Quintas?" Sir Hughes said, his eyes straight ahead, scanning the desert.

"I see them," Quintas answered. My lack of sleep and the illness that had overcome me in the chamber left me functioning at less than peak efficiency. I glanced to my left and observed a group of raiders trailing us far across the valley floor. They were a large force, nearly thirty in number. Sir Hughes and Quintas had noticed them almost immediately. The raiders were trailing us far to our left, near the foothills, but Sir Hughes gave no indication that they had been seen. He kept us riding forward across the valley floor. Until he was ready to face them.

"Halt," Sir Hughes said.

We reined to a stop and turned our mounts to face them. As we waited, our lances pointed skyward, Sir Hughes looked at me through the eye slit of his helmet.

"Young Borneo," he said. "Are you ready?"

"Ready for what, Sir Hughes?"

"Battle," he replied. Without warning, he lowered his lance, spurred his horse and charged toward their line. Quintas and I both shouted in unison, not a war cry but in surprise. We three alone had never faced so large a force.

The raiders were surprised and at first watched in amazement as these three crazed knights and a single dog bolted across the desert floor toward them. They recovered quickly and spurred their own mounts toward us. Surely we were doomed. We were outnumbered more than ten to one.

As the first raider reached Sir Hughes, he drove his lance into the man, driving him from the saddle. And as he rode among them, he took the reins in his teeth, drew his sword and struck down two more. And as he cleared their line, three men descended on him.

He disappeared.

The men were confused as his riderless horse galloped away from them. Once it was past them, Sir Hughes was suddenly on its back again. He reined the horse around and rode back into them, hacking away with his sword. The three men fell to the ground mortally wounded.

I do not know if Quintas saw what I saw, but many of the raiders did. They shouted in confusion. A small group of them had not witnessed this miraculous event, though. They came charging straight in my direction. I took down the lead rider with my lance. The second died the same way.

But the next four riders were nearly upon me. I screamed and drew my sword, ready to die.

Instead, just like Sir Hughes, I disappeared.

Secrets

When we returned to the temple that night, Sir Hughes explained to Quintas what had happened. But he did not take him to the chamber. Quintas was a devout and holy man and the three of us agreed to keep the existence of the Grail a secret. I think in truth a part of him was afraid to be exposed to it.

Quintas was also a clever man. If he were alive now I think he would be an engineer or inventor of some type. He was our X-Ray, always experimenting with weapons and the devices of the day, trying to find ways to make them better. When we described what we'd uncovered in the chamber and told him that the Grail was secreted behind lead, he was curious. In the Middle Ages lead was rarely used except as weights, anchors, that sort of thing. Quintas worked with the armorers in Jerusalem, the men who made and repaired our weapons. He knew that when you added a small amount of molten copper to melted lead, the resulting alloy gained strength and was resistant to corrosion.

He deduced that those who had guarded the Grail had chosen a plate of lead treated with copper to shield the Grail from the elements. Whether by luck or plan, the plate had also prevented the cup's light from shining through it. But Croc had probably pawed it loose and we were unintentionally exposed to its power.

Sir Hughes decided that the Grail should be ready to be moved at a moment's notice. If Jerusalem were overrun, leaving it in the Temple was far too dangerous. He tasked Quintas with building a container that would be portable, yet keep it safe. Furthermore, he decided that I would be the one to carry it to safety.

"There is no better rider in our group," he said. "If all is lost, you must take it to a place where it will be safe."

Quintas worked on this container while the rest of us fought. Sir Hughes carefully used our newfound power to build up our legend. We learned to control it. Not only that, we were soon able to blink further distances. And in doing so, Sir Hughes turned our ability into a powerful recruiting tool.

"You and I together are like one hundred knights," he said. And indeed he was right. We would ride into the camps of our enemies and disappear before their eyes, reappearing behind them to strike them down. We would attack a small group of bandits, and a few moments later attack another force miles away. We would suddenly appear in the middle of their camp–always on foot because we could never blink with the horses–which made it seem the Templars were everywhere at once.

"When word of our victories spread, more knights will

flock to our cause. Watch. You'll see," he said.

He was right. Before long dozens, then hundreds of knights arrived in Jerusalem requesting to join the Order. Sir Hughes became the first grand master of the Knights Templar. We sent the original members back to Europe and recruited more knights, and the Order's power and influence grew. In two years' time, we were one of the most powerful and fearsome fighting forces in history.

Quintas invented an ingenious container to hold the Grail. It was a wooden cylinder, lined with lead. But the crowning achievement was the intricate combination he created as part of its design. One night he asked to measure my hands.

"My hands?" I said.

"Don't ask questions. Put your hands on the parchment," he said. Quintas could be bossy when he was working on his projects. Again, he reminded me a great deal of X-Ray.

He traced my hands with a quill dipped in ink. He was careful and meticulous.

"What are you doing?" I asked.

"You'll see," Quintas said. Done with his tracing, he blew the ink dry and scurried away.

A few weeks later, he summoned Sir Hughes to our quarters. It was late at night, but since our ranks had grown, there were often brother knights coming and going at all hours. We spoke in whispers.

"Something so valuable must have extra levels of protection," Quintas said. From a cloth bag he removed the container. At the time I'd never seen anything so beautiful. It had been carved from the trunk of a pistachio tree, which is a notoriously hard wood. But somehow he found a way to carve carefully constructed grooves within it. It must have taken him hundreds of hours. He handed it to me. On top of one end he had carved the Templar seal.

"Place your left hand over the seal and your fingers in the grooves. The seal always goes in the palm of your left hand. Your right hand will fit in the grooves on the other side," he said.

"Amazing, Quintas—you made this specifically for young Borneo?" Sir Hughes asked.

"Yes," Quintas answered, with just a small measure of pride in his voice.

"Stunning," he said.

"What are these rings in the middle?" I asked. There were sixteen wooden rings surrounding the cylinder. Each with a series of numbers carved into it.

"Ah," Quintas said. "The best part. There are sixteen wooden rings. Essentially the container is a series of cylinders within cylinders that rotate inside. When they are moved in the right sequence they will open a series of locks. They must be rotated properly in sequence. Then your hands must apply the right amount of pressure. Turn your left hand to the right and your right hand to the left and the cylinder will open. It requires both the correct combination *and* the pressure. And it is made for your hands alone. Once the Grail is sealed inside only you will be able to open it, young Borneo," he said.

"What if someone tries to break it open? With an axe or by burning the wood?" I asked.

Quintas shrugged. "I can only do what I can do. We must

keep it hidden, but it cannot be opened by anyone but young Borneo unless they know the combination and have hands exactly the same size as his. Pistachio wood is extremely hard, difficult to burn. I suppose someone could smash it open. But it is obviously holding something valuable. Would anyone take the chance on breaking it open and perhaps also destroying what is inside? I cannot answer that question. I will carve a message in the side with a stern warning that opening it by force will damage what it holds."

"And you have done more than I could have imagined, Quintas," Sir Hughes said.

Every night, before we went to sleep, Quintas would drill me on the use of the container. I practiced and practiced until the combination and feel of the container was seared into my brain. Quintas's design worked perfectly.

As it turns out, he completed it just in time. Two weeks later a large force of Saracens besieged Jerusalem. It was time to move it to safety.

But the Grail held still more secrets. Because before the siege we also learned the Grail had the power to heal. And it is most likely because of that power that I am sitting here today.

The Miracle

Before the city was besieged, Sir Hughes and I rode out on patrol. I had taken to leaving Croc behind at the Temple to safeguard the hidden room. Even before he lived a thousand years he was an uncommonly smart dog. If anyone showed interest in the chamber he would blink to us right away and we would return to make sure nothing was disturbed.

Not far outside the city, we found a group of raiders harassing a small band of pilgrims. As they rode down upon us, we disappeared and reappeared behind, around, and in front of them, steadily reducing their number. Still they held firm, waiting patiently for us to reappear; then they would attack.

It was our first indication that the blink had limits. All that week we had been fighting as the numbers of our enemies grew. We had used the power a great deal within a short period of time. The longer the distance traveled, the more frequent the use of the power, the longer it took us to blink again. I discovered it first. I reappeared in front of one of the raiders and his scimitar whistled through the air, slicing through my tunic. Luckily the chain mail beneath it protected me from injury. He swung again and I parried with my blade and tried to blink away. But I stayed where I was.

"Sir Hughes!" I shouted. "Something . . . is wrong!" I could barely speak as this raider closed on me, swinging his giant weapon back and forth, nearly taking my head off a half dozen times.

"Steady now, young Borneo," he shouted. Sir Hughes fought his way toward me, striking down two men with his sword. We were caught in a morass of bodies, horses, and shouting, grunting men. Our one tactical advantage was lost, and we were outnumbered and about to die. Had the power of the Grail deserted us?

Somehow he finally fought his way to my side. The next thing I remember is Sir Hughes grabbing me by the arm and we blinked away. Not far, but close enough to where we had left our horses that we could stagger to them and mount up. We turned and rode toward the city with the remaining raiders hot on our heels.

At first, I could scarcely hold on to the reins. I was worried I would tumble from the saddle. Sir Hughes must have noticed.

"Hold on, young Borneo," he shouted over the thundering hooves. "Hold on."

The raiders were closing fast. Try as I might, I could not blink. Sir Hughes maneuvered his horse next to mine, only inches separating us. He reached out, grasping my arm.

I did not know it was possible for Sir Hughes to "carry" me when he blinked. But I came to on the floor of the chamber where the Grail was hidden, and Croc was licking my face. Sir Hughes lay next to me, groaning in pain. I clambered to my hands and knees.

"Sir . . . Hughes," I stammered. "Are you . . ."

Blood soaked through his tunic. He gasped for air.

"Young . . . Borneo," he croaked.

"How did you . . . You brought us here?"

"Yes."

"What happened?"

He tried to sit up, but he was too weak.

"I have learned its powers, young Borneo. At first, I thought we uncovered the power God granted to St. Ignatius."

"St. Ignatius?" I couldn't think. As I've said, I was not devout and I struggled to recall the miracle of St. Ignatius.

Sir Hughes chuckled and coughed, making a horrible wheezing sound. "You should have paid more attention at church, lad. Bi-location. St. Ignatius had the power to appear in two places at once." He put his hand to his side. When he lifted it away, it was covered in blood. "I believe I grew too bold in our last engagement, young Borneo. It would appear a raider's arrow found its mark before I could blink us away."

His body shuddered and shook with spasms there on the floor. I sensed he was near the end. Croc was whimpering and continued licking my face. I felt something warm and wet on my forehead. Touching it, I found I was bleeding from a scalp wound. Sir Hughes wheezed.

"I have studied our gift. It is the gift of speed. We simply move faster than it is possible for human eyes to see. I don't know if this is what God intended when he granted us this power. And as you saw today–" He was racked by a coughing fit.

"Sir Hughes, you must let me take you to the physician," I said. "Please."

"No! No, young Borneo. You . . ."

He lost consciousness. Croc whimpered and nudged his body with his snout. My eyes filled with blood from the wound on my forehead. I wiped it away and shook him.

"Sir Hughes! Sir Hughes," I shouted. But he did not wake up.

Then the strange noise we'd heard the first night we discovered the Grail started up again. Croc barked and went to the wall, rising on his hind legs and pawing at the lead panel. I stood and rushed to it, quickly using my dagger to pry it loose. The light burst out of the small alcove, its blue glow filling the chamber.

I took the Grail in my hands and held it. The weakness and pain I felt were instantly gone. I touched my head wound to find the skin smooth and unbroken. But when I held out the Grail and bathed Sir Hughes in its light, it did not cure his wounds or restore him to life. Like all things in this world, it apparently had its limits.

Not knowing what else to do, I hurried to my quarters and retrieved the container Quintas had so brilliantly designed. Returning to the chamber I put the Grail inside it. I prayed over Sir Hughes's body, then sealed him up inside the chamber. In some way I felt he would have been pleased to rest there for eternity.

That night, I gathered up my equipment and I rode out

of Jerusalem. The Saracen forces were gathering in the hills. I did not wish to be trapped there with something so valuable. I could not risk it falling into the wrong hands.

In time I learned to master the blink. As did Croc. It had the power to heal, but it did not grant immortality. I'm aging, but at a very slow rate. Sir Hughes died and the Grail could not bring him back. I did not get a chance to study it, to find out what other powers it can or cannot grant us.

For not long after I left Jerusalem it was taken from me.

And I've been looking for it ever since. For nearly a thousand years I have never stopped looking for it. Now I finally know who has it. It is all clear to me. I understand now what needs to be done. We must find it.

We must end this.

MONDAY, SEPTEMBER 15 >

2:30 p.m. to 5:00 p.m. PST

Lost and Found

Angela turned off the recorder.

"You lost it?" Angela said. "How?"

We'd been listening to Boone and I had found it hard to breathe. The Holy Grail? Was that even possible? Boone stared out at the water, saying nothing. It was as if some big burden had been lifted off of his shoulders. I couldn't imagine it.

"Uh. Boone," I said. "You realize that ever since Kitty Hawk we've known you can *poof!* or blink or whatever you call it, and it's been driving us both nuts. Could you finish the story?" I said.

"Sorry. It's just so strange. The two of you are the first people I've talked about this with in . . . centuries."

"You lost it," Angela prodded him.

Boone still sat quietly.

"Boone, I know this must be hard," Angela said. "But you have to tell us. You need to trust us. My mom is still pretending to be the Leopard. Number One is still out there. We are still in danger. If something happens, we need to know what to do."

"I know. You're right, as usual, Angela. But both of you need to promise me that you will never tell another soul what I'm about to tell you. Not even your parents. You can't reveal this knowledge to anyone," Boone said.

"Boone," I said, trying and failing to keep the incredulity out of my voice. "I think that's the least of your worries. Can't you see how that conversation would go? 'Mom, Roger, please sit down. Angela and I have something to tell you about Boone. Apparently he's been alive for almost a thousand years, and he can blink around all over the place at the speed of light. Also, he was a Knight Templar and found the Holy Grail, and there's some other weird stuff, too, that we'll get to later. Just wanted you to know. Please pass the kale.'

"Forget about sending us to Haversham Boarding Academy. They'd be sending us to a completely different kind of school. A special school where people walk around in funny jackets. So I don't think you need to worry about Angela and me keeping your secret."

Boone laughed. "Point taken. You're quite the comedian, Q."

"I didn't used to be. Not until I tripped over you outside the coach in the desert. I used to keep my thoughts to myself. Maybe a quirky observation once in a while. But now my nerves are shot, and I can't shut up."

Boone smiled. "I know. You've been through a lot, and most of it has been my fault. I want you both to know I'm sorry for that."

He took a deep breath.

"I rode out of Jerusalem. Part of me felt like a deserter. I'd left my fellow knights in the city, facing a large enemy force. But I had a greater duty. I had my horse and Croc and I had the Grail. My goal was to find someplace to keep it safe. Where no one would ever find it. But where would that be?

"I rode north toward Acre. I thought perhaps I could return to Italy and hide it somewhere on my father's estate. Maybe I would take it to Rome and let the pope deal with it, though my instinct warned me against that.

"Halfway to Acre, I needed supplies. I stopped at a small village to buy provisions and to rest my horse. The next night, I camped in the hills a day's ride from the village. Ten bandits ambushed me. One of them clubbed me in the face with a mace. I was seriously wounded."

"I don't understand," I said. "How come you just didn't blink away?"

"Because ever since that day in the desert, when Hughes and I were unable to blink, I had refrained from using the power. I was scared of it. I didn't understand yet how long it took me to regenerate. They came at us from downwind. Croc did not smell them in time to warn me. They got lucky. Though I was wounded, I realized if I didn't use the power I would die. So I used it again. My life was at stake. I fought them off. They took my horse, a few of my weapons, but I was hurt and bleeding. Even Croc had been injured."

"You used the Grail," Angela said. "To heal yourself."

Boone nodded. "I didn't know what else to do. If I died there, someone would find it. They might not know what they had, they might not be able to open it, but I could not risk it. As I had rehearsed it so many times, I moved the numbers in sequence and applied the pressure. The container clicked open and as I removed the Grail, the light washed over Croc and me. But . . ."

"But there was someone else there," Angela said.

Boone nodded.

"How do you know all this stuff, brainiac?" I asked.

"Because he said he lost it. Simple deduction—he was wounded, healing but not fully healed, and someone came along and took it before he was strong enough to stop them," she said. Angela was never happier than when she was solving a puzzle, doing extra homework, or helping bring down an international terrorist organization. Figuring out what happened to a sacred relic was making her positively giddy.

"Angela is right," Boone said. "As the light glowed from the Grail, a young boy, perhaps ten or twelve years old, appeared from the underbrush and was bathed in the light of the Grail as well. His sudden appearance startled me. I had only a moment to close the container. I got it closed, but he grabbed it and ran off. The only thing I know about him is that he was a native of the region and he carried a kithara over his shoulder. We tried to follow him; Croc tracked him for miles, but eventually he lost the scent."

"Speed," Angela said. Now she was just showing off.

"What's a kithara?" I asked. "Isn't that a country?"

"No, that's Qatar," Boone said. "A kithara is an early version of the guitar. A popular instrument in those days."

"And you think that kid was my . . . was Speed?" I said.

"Yes," Boone said. "Once you found the feather, a couple of things clicked into place for me. When you saw him on the highway on the way to Kitty Hawk, he was driving. My guess is he blinked all the way across the country and he was too low on juice to blink anywhere else, so he had to use a car. Then I started thinking about it. His rock-star persona is the perfect cover. His background—his money and access—it all fits the profile of the other ghost cell members. Add in the fact that X-Ray discovered his birth records are so sketchy. He's an orphan all right, only his real parents died centuries ago. Just like mine."

"And he's been using his musical persona as a cover, just like you did as a roadie," I said.

"Yes," Boone said.

"And you never died?" Angela said.

"No. I didn't die. I've aged. So has Speed. He was a young boy, now he's in his forties. I was in my twenties and now I'm in my . . . I'm older," Boone said. "Speed was exposed to the light of the Grail. Just enough to give him the power. But what he saw . . . he knows how valuable it is. But he can't figure out how to open it. Even after all these years he can't be sure exactly what is inside the container. He's too smart to try and pry it open or cut it open or use some other method for fear he might damage it."

We were all quiet a minute, trying to let it all sink in.

"But I have a question," I said. "Why did I blink in Chicago? On the roof?"

Boone shrugged. "I don't know, Q. The easy answer is, you're Speed's son so it was passed down to you. Maybe not the full power but some of it. I never married or had children, so I don't know if a child of mine would do the same thing you did under the same conditions. But my guess is that somehow, this light . . . it's like some form of radiation or something. I'm not a scientist, but it has to have altered our DNA or something. If it did fundamentally change us at the cellular level, then it only makes sense there's a chance we'd pass it on to our children, just like you could pass on any genetic trait such as red hair or blue eyes."

I thought about that. I guess Speed did give me something besides headaches and bad memories. He probably never intended to do it, but he passed it on to me nonetheless.

"Something else that bothers me," Angela said. "If there were other people, like priests, protecting it, why didn't they get the same ability? Why didn't they live forever like you and blink and all the rest?"

Boone shrugged. "I don't know that they didn't. Maybe there are others out there like us. My guess, though, is that somehow, if the Grail gave them the power, they either died, like Sir Hughes, or . . . I've been thinking about it for a thousand years and I just don't have all the answers."

"So what do we do now?" I asked.

"We wait. And hope Buddy finds what I've been looking for the last one thousand years."

Discovery

"There is enough intelligence in this single safe-deposit box to destroy half the terrorist cells in the entire world," Eben said. He had found a small plastic box full of flash drives. All of them were encrypted, but X-Ray had provided him with a small tablet device that ran decryption software, allowing him to quickly review the contents of each device.

"You remember what I gave you, and tell Boone I cooperated when this is all over," Buddy said.

"After this is over, Mr. T., you will be fortunate if I do not shoot you myself," Eben said.

"But . . . you can't . . . you . . . there are laws," Buddy stammered. The later it became, the more of a mess Buddy was becoming.

Eben shrugged. "I am not an American citizen. I am a citizen of Israel who also happens to have diplomatic immunity. When this is over, and if I so choose, I can shoot you. And return to Israel and the bosom of my family without any interference from the U.S. government."

Buddy's face grew white, and beads of perspiration formed on his forehead.

"No . . . no . . . you can't. Diplomatic immunity doesn't cover murder," Buddy mumbled.

Eben removed the flash drive from the tablet and dropped it in the open duffel bag.

"Who said anything about murder? It would be a clear case of self-defense," he said, beaming a big smile at Buddy.

"There's no box here, Buddy," Malak said harshly, still pretending to be Anmar the Leopard. She had been watching the exchange in silence. She had also come to the conclusion that she liked Eben Lavi a lot.

"I *told* you," Buddy said. "I don't know where it is. If he says I have it, then it's got to be in one of these places."

"I hope you are not wrong, Buddy. For your sake," Malak said.

They loaded all of the flash drives and even some old floppy disks into the duffel bag. It made Malak and Eben wonder about just how long the ghost cell had been active. Malak looked at her watch.

"I don't get it, Buddy said. "You're the Leopard, and you're Mossad. Why haven't you . . . you know . . . killed each other?"

Malak and Eben looked at each other. Earlier they had discussed how to play it if Buddy tried to weasel his way out of trouble. Or perhaps play one of them against the other. Buddy was a deal maker. There was always the chance he would try to form some kind of alliance and try to bluff or buy his way out of the vise he was currently squeezed in. They had agreed to pretend they had reached a temporary truce, with an underlying level of thinly veiled contempt.

"I have hunted the Leopard for many years," Eben said. "But this is a case of how, as you Americans say, 'the enemy of my enemy is also my enemy.' "

"That's not what we—" Buddy said, but Eben interrupted him.

"Enough, Mr. Buddy T. Do not worry about my feelings for the Leopard. When you are safely locked away, she will receive my full attention."

"Listen to the great Mossad agent," Malak sneered. "I have been right under your nose a dozen times and you have never so much as gotten a glimpse of me. Once this is done, I will disappear, like a leopard in the grass. You will never see me again. Until I come for you."

Buddy watched their exchange and blanched, realizing that getting them angry was making him nervous. He gulped and looked down at the floor. Malak and Eben discreetly smiled at each other.

"We have enough time to visit one last bank. Think hard. Where is the next place you have boxes big enough to hold what Number One described to you?"

Buddy looked over the list of banks.

"National Standard Bank," Buddy said.

Malak snatched the paper from his hand, then glanced at her watch.

"For your sake, you had better hope you are right. I am not as patient as Boone."

The three of them left the building and piled into the

intellimobile. Vanessa deftly maneuvered it through the city traffic, and they pulled up in front of the bank. Malak, Eben, and Buddy entered and repeated the same procedure to sign in to the vault as they had at every other location.

Buddy had three safe-deposit boxes at this site. They found the container Number One was looking for inside the second one. They emptied the contents of the other two into a bag, then stared at the metal case.

"That's got to be it," Buddy said. "It looks exactly like how he described it to me!"

"Finally," Eben said. "I wonder what it could be that has your Number One so anxious to get his hands on it."

"Who cares!" Buddy said. "Let's just get it to him! Then you can catch him."

The metal case was heavy and latched shut. Flipping it open, they saw a wooden cylinder lying in a piece of cut-out foam. It had many wooden rings encircling it, with numbers carved into the rings. It looked very old.

Malak grabbed Buddy T. firmly by the arm. She squeezed. Hard.

"Oww. Oww!" Buddy yelped.

"What is in the wooden container, Mr. T.?" she demanded.

"Oww. Let go! I don't know! I swear I don't know!" Buddy cried.

She released his arm.

"How did an imbecile like you rise so far in the vaunted ghost cell?"

Buddy didn't answer, he just rubbed his sore arm.

She closed the heavy case and took it in one hand and

grabbed Buddy by the other.

Eben followed behind as they exited the building.

Takedown

Speed Paulsen had just woken up from a nap and was relaxing on the couch in his living room. As he sat, he quietly strummed a Washburn guitar he had bought at auction. Playing the guitar calmed him down. It once belonged to Bob Marley. He liked to collect guitars from other great guitar players, especially those no longer living. Marley was a good guitarist, but not as good as Speed. The Washburn was a fine instrument, though. One of his favorites. His fingers were moving back and forth, progressing through the chords, when a beep from the computer monitor interrupted him.

After his interrogation of Buddy, he'd sent his best men with him to get the item. He came home to sleep and rest. He could only use his ability over short distances. He referred to it as "speeding." He'd been using it a lot the last few days. He needed to recharge.

The three apartments were on the top floor of the building facing west, toward the bay. He spent most of his time in the middle one and now climbed through a hidden door in the bedroom closet and entered the master suite of the adjacent apartment. It was filled with computer monitors. Buddy thought he had secrets from Number One, but nothing Buddy did was secret. Speed knew every move he made. He pulled up the logs of activity reports from his various teams on his computer screen.

Strange. The team he'd sent with Buddy had not reported in for some time. He pulled up a program that would ping the transponder in their van. There was no signal. Punching keys on the keyboard he tracked their progress. They had taken Buddy from the warehouse to a bank downtown. After that the signal disappeared. And there was no word from the countersurveillance teams at that location either.

Something had gone wrong.

Once he captured Buddy, he had countersurveillance teams following him. All of their vehicles were equipped with video cameras and sent recordings back to his monitors here in the apartment. He could easily track their movements.

He cycled back to the recording until he found what he was looking for. On one of the large monitors above him, three people were entering a bank. Speed sat up. One of the men looked vaguely familiar. What was Buddy up to? Perhaps he'd hired bodyguards or someone he thought could protect him from Number One? Then he looked at the third person and jumped up from his seat.

It was Anmar! The traitor. What was she doing here? He had carefully planned for her demise in Chicago. He had visited the safe house and left her the envelope with the instructions. He had called her and sent her to Grant Park.

She would be dead if Buddy hadn't botched things. But she should have disappeared. Why was she with Buddy T.? How had Buddy managed to involve the Leopard?

Speed tried to process it quickly.

Anmar must somehow have learned of the foiled attack in Chicago and their plans to kill her. It would not have been a great leap for her to deduce their plans for her body to be discovered among the dead and blamed for the attacks. Yet she had not gone to ground. The Leopard was a hunter. But how could she have made the connection to Buddy T.? The Leopard was good. But she was not that good.

Speed sat back and closed his eyes, thinking hard. After a moment he believed he had the answer. Buddy T. was the only other person in the ghost cell who knew Anmar was in the safe house. It had been Buddy T. who had first called her on the phone. Once the Chicago op had been botched, Buddy was most likely worried that his life was in danger. He was a coward by nature and he must have realized Speed would want answers for what had gone wrong. He might have even worried that Speed would kill him.

He wasn't wrong.

Somehow, after he captured Buddy and demanded the return of the item, Buddy made contact with the Leopard. Or more likely, the Leopard had tracked down Buddy and taken out his team. Buddy must have convinced her Speed was the one she wanted and that he could lead her to him. It was the only reason Speed could think of that would keep the Leopard from killing Buddy on the spot. He had made a bargain. If she spared his life, he would lead her to the one who had really ordered her death.

The Leopard's honor would not let her refuse such an offer. Buddy didn't know it but even if the Leopard succeeded in killing Number One, she would certainly kill him afterward. That's who she was. A killer.

Still. Something smelled.

How had she made it to San Francisco so quickly? And who were these other people? As far as he knew, the Leopard worked alone. Were these others a crew Buddy had hired?

Boone.

Boone had been involved the whole time. Speed had already figured out that Boone was the one from whom he had taken the object all those years ago—the wounded knight on the battlefield. When he had gone to supervise the kidnapping of Bethany Culpepper and ran into Boone following on the highway in the tour bus, he'd grown suspicious. Knowing Boone as a roadie from his years in the music business, Speed had heard all the rumors. People said Boone was really a spy. That he had been involved in the intelligence game for years. Speed himself had never believed it. Boone was as incompetent as Speed was brilliant. Yet there he had been, right in the middle of the kidnapping, traveling in the same direction as his cell members. So he played his dumb Speed act, and let Boone think he had the upper hand. He knew Angela and Q had ditched him in the hospital. So he had "sped" after them. He had watched the entire thing go down at Kitty Hawk and he had nearly burst when he saw Boone do the same thing he could do! After all these years he had found the Last Templar! And to think all along it had been Tyrone

Boone.

Tyrone Boone. Ever since Kitty Hawk, he had been playing Boone until he could maneuver him into place. Everything he had done after Kitty Hawk had been designed to keep Boone guessing and draw him here, to the object. Once Buddy retrieved it, he would find a way to persuade Boone to open the container.

He knew Boone had others working for him, but Boone was careful. He kept his people out of sight. Whether it was Buddy who contacted Anmar or Boone had somehow persuaded her to join him in finding Number One, it didn't matter. They had overplayed their hand. Speed Paulsen set the agenda. Speed Paulsen was in charge here. He would get what he wanted.

He always got what he wanted.

And then he would kill them all.

Now somehow Buddy or Boone had brought in Anmar the traitor. Could she have been working for Boone all along? He looked at the monitor again. The other man she was with. Where had he seen him before?

Boone. Anmar. The kidnapping. Kitty Hawk.

Speed punched a few more keys and pulled up the footage of the raid on the house on Kitty Hawk. Where Number Four had ultimately died. He watched as two agents burst through the front door and Anmar grabbed Number Four, pulling him to his feet. He isolated the image of one of the agents. It was the same man who was with Anmar now.

He let the footage play again, watching as Anmar shot the two agents, but hitting them solidly where their bulletproof vests would protect them. Now one of those men was here. It had all been an act. Anmar had been working with Boone, or at least for U.S. Intelligence, for some time.

As he thought about it, it made sense. Boone had the resources, the access to intelligence. Buddy T. was a coward. He would never have tried to make a deal with the Leopard. He would have approached Boone. And Boone must have been working with the Leopard the whole time.

How had he missed it? He'd suspected she was a traitor. In Chicago, he had ordered her death. But Boone had somehow interfered.

And right now Buddy was being handled by Boone's people. Boone. That old geezer thought he could still pull a fast one on Speed Paulsen. You had to give the guy credit. He didn't give up. After all these years, he had been looking for Speed. Wanting to recover what Speed had taken from him.

"I've been right under your nose, old man," Speed chuckled to himself. "What a loser."

Speed closed his eyes and looked at all the angles. The Leopard was a twist he had not expected. Though she had betrayed the cause she was a killer and she was dangerous. What if Buddy T. had cracked and told them who he was?

He laughed out loud. It doesn't matter what they know. Or how they know it. They are all going to die. Today.

All that mattered was that Anmar was carrying *the* case. It held the object. Buddy T. had done it. No matter how he'd screwed things up by bringing in Boone and Anmar, the case had been found. That was the main thing.

Everything had fallen into place. By tonight, he could

be on his way. He spun around in the chair in front of the monitor. He sat in silence a moment, taking time to think. Had he considered everything? Yes. There was not a single flaw in his plan.

He closed his eyes and vanished.

Only the chair, spinning slightly in the now-empty room, remained.

Out of Nowhere

The intellimobile was parked at the curb. Vanessa and X-Ray were standing on the sidewalk in front of it. The side door was open. It was the same procedure they had used at each bank. They hustled Buddy out and into the van and drove off.

Malak couldn't identify what it was that made her feel like something was wrong. As always, she was wearing her sunglasses. She kept her head straight ahead while her eyes darted everywhere, making threat assessments. Nothing looked out of the ordinary. But her skin tingled and the hairs on the back of her neck were standing at attention.

Down the street a telephone worker stood inside a lift, working on a telephone line high up the pole. A delivery truck was parked across the street, but the driver was nowhere to be seen. Could they be cell members spying on them? Reporting back to Number One on their activities?

Thinking there might be a sniper, she scanned the rooftops across the street. But nothing looked suspicious. Why did it feel like something was wrong? Time seemed to slow down. In her mind, the distance to the van grew, as if it were at the end of a long tunnel. With each step, it appeared to draw farther away from them instead of closer. Malak released Buddy's arm and put her hand on the grip of her pistol beneath her jacket.

"Eben," she whispered. "Be alert. Something isn't right."

Malak had the same feeling she'd felt back in the Chicago safe house. Someone was watching her. But who? The few people in the street around them did not look dangerous. Nor were any of them paying attention to the team. Something or someone was toying with her, as if they were standing just at the edge of her vision. Yet she was unable to pinpoint the source of her unease, could not see who was watching. Eben did not ask questions. He put his hand into his pocket immediately.

The attack did not come until they had almost arrived at the intellimobile. Malak could not grasp what was happening at first: Buddy made a quiet gasping sound and slumped to his knees before falling to the ground. At first she thought he'd been shot, but blood flowered on the back of his shirt and she realized he'd been stabbed.

"Eben—"

Her words were cut off as a piercing pain struck her in the thigh, collapsing her leg. She cried out and tried to draw her gun, but something sharp slashed across her arm, and she was unable to move it. Vanessa drew one of her throwing knives immediately and moved forward toward Malak, who tried to shove the case to her with her remaining good arm. Then Vanessa doubled over, dropping to her knees and clutching her stomach. Blood seeped through her fingers. X-Ray tried to pull a gun from his jacket, but a vicious cut appeared across his hand, and the pistol tumbled to the pavement.

"Eben!" Malak tried to shout, but it emerged from her throat as a croak. "The case."

Eben darted forward, reaching for it, but he cried out as a cut appeared across his coat sleeve. "Ahh!" he howled. But he did not stop, taking still another step, reaching for the case Malak held clutched in her hand. Then he was down, clawing at the hamstring of his left leg. There was blood everywhere.

"No!" Malak screamed. "No!"

She felt herself falling and tried to throw her body over the case, hoping to protect it somehow until help arrived. But her head spun with dizziness, her body weakened, and she landed on the concrete beside it, though her hand still grasped the handle. Then the case was suddenly gone. It had been right there in her hand and it just disappeared before her eyes. Despite feeling woozy and lightheaded from blood loss, she was certain no one had taken it. It just vanished.

With her good arm, she pushed herself up until she could flip over on her back. She tried to pull out her cell phone but could only claw weakly at her pocket. Her vision began to narrow. A shadow crossed over her face, and she looked up to see Ziv standing above her, his gun in his hand. Ziv, the Monkey, always watching but never seen, had appeared at her side. From somewhere far off in the distance, she heard the sounds of screaming and running feet, and farther away the noise of sirens drawing closer.

"Malak," he said. Then he gasped in pain, throwing his head back. He slumped to the ground.

"Ziv," she hissed, her breath coming in ragged gasps. With his last bit of strength, he threw himself across her. The Monkey still protecting the Leopard.

The Beginning of the End

"Boone? How do you learn to control it? The power?" I asked.

"It's hard to explain, Q. When I think back on it, I realize that at first I could only use it when I was experiencing strong emotions. Fear, anxiety, excitement. You feel all of those in battle. That first night in the room where we found it, I blinked because I was nervous and excited. Eventually it's like learning to control your temper or any other feeling. With practice you gain control over it. After a time, the sickness and nausea go away. But it is important to remember it does have limits. I can't blink through solid walls or doors. I need an opening. I can't blink with someone who doesn't have the same ability. For instance, I couldn't take Angela by the hand and blink her across the bay. And the greater the distance and the more often you blink, the more time it takes you to recover," Boone said. "And like I said, in the last few years it's taking Croc and me both a lot longer to regenerate."

"Maybe that's why it happened to me. I was terrified when I saw that Angela was about to be shot. And is that why, when you showed up at the John Hancock building in Chicago, you looked like a boiled fish? Because you'd been using it so much?" I asked.

"Yes. I had been in the park, moving fast and looking for anything nearby that might be a threat. Basically, I'd been blinking all morning. When I got the call and met you there, I was almost out of juice. But for some reason Croc seems to regenerate faster than I do. That's how he was able to get the device to X-Ray and come back and help you get out of the building," Boone said.

"So Speed passed it on to Q," Angela said. She had that look on her face like she was really concentrating, trying to take it all in and figure it out. "And you said you never had children, right?"

Boone nodded. "That's right. I dedicated my life to finding the Grail. When you are a soldier there is no worse feeling than thinking you've failed in your last assignment. So to answer your question, Angela, no. I never had a family. Never married or had children. I felt it would not be fair to them. I had to devote myself to a greater cause."

Boone looked at her with sad eyes. "Much like what your mother did. I'm not sure I could have done it. But it's no exaggeration to say she's saved hundreds, if not thousands, of lives."

Angela was quiet, biting her lower lip. But I guess she didn't know what to say, because she remained silent.

"So you think I blinked because Speed is my dad?" I muttered. I couldn't help it. The only thing the guy had ever given me in my entire life was something that made me throw up when I used it. Although there was a small part of me that was a little excited about the fact that I had this ability. Even if I hadn't learned how to use it yet, I couldn't help but think of the magic tricks I could do with it. And whenever Roger served another salad, I could blink to Burger King and he'd be none the wiser. Whoa. Racing mind again.

"Boone, do you think Speed suspects you're on to him, and that's why he's making Buddy retrieve the Grail?" Angela said. "Will he disappear and you'll have to start all over again?"

"I think he's going to make a play. If he hasn't figured it all out yet, he's very close to doing so. And he knows if he can unlock the power of it he'll be unstoppable," Boone said. "He's run one of the most successful terrorist organizations in human history. I think he's had eyes on Buddy T. the entire time, maybe with some tracking device or surveillance even X-Ray can't detect. It wouldn't surprise me if he was there on the island at Kitty Hawk, if he had enough time to regenerate. And he knows we're closing in. Besides—"

The chirp of Boone's phone interrupted them. It was sitting on the table. He pressed the speakerphone button.

"Go, Pat," he said.

"Boone, we got trouble. The whole team got taken down outside a bank downtown."

Angela sat up. "My mom."

"Angela?" Callaghan said. "They're in ambulances on the way to San Francisco General. She was injured. I don't know how badly. Vanessa was seriously hurt. It's bad, Boone. I got a buddy at SFPD to send me the footage from a security camera outside the bank. I'm sending you the video. The video . . .

Boone—it's bad."

"Oh, God," Boone murmured as he looked at his phone screen. "It happened." His face was ashen.

"What was that?" Pat's voice came over the phone. "Boone, repeat."

"It was nothing." Boone took a breath. "Okay. Pat, you get to the hospital. Use your Secret Service credentials and get the entire team in a single OR ward so they can all be treated together. Seal it up tight. Keep all the doctors and nurses inside. And I mean *tight*. Doors locked and no windows open. There can't be any way in or out of that room until you hear from me."

"Boone, what are you—"

"There's no time, Pat. Trust me. You use any means necessary to execute this order. Copy?"

"I copy," Pat said.

"Get Felix to the site, have him secure the intellimobile. Leave Uly here to run countersurveillance on the boat. Felix is to return here once he has the intellimobile. Once he's back, he and Uly don't let Angela and Q out of their sight. Do you understand?"

"All right, Boone," Callaghan said. "It's your play. What are you going to be doing?"

"Just call me when you reach the hospital," Boone said, disconnecting before Callaghan could answer.

"I'm not staying here." Angela was standing up now. "You have to take me to my mother."

"Angela, I can't," Boone said. "Speed has figured it out. He knows who I am. Who I really am. And if he knows that, there's a good chance he thinks I know how to open it. And to get me to do that he's going to try to get some leverage, something to trade. I think he might come after you or Q again. I have to keep you someplace safe."

"Boone! I'm going to my mother!" Angela was insistent.

"Angela!" I said. "Boone's right. Let him do his job. The best thing you can do for your mom is stay safe."

Angela slumped back in her seat, the energy drained out of her.

"I'm not sure how much longer I can take this," she said.

Boone put his hand on her shoulder. "I know you've been through a lot. But you *can* do this. Just hang in a little while longer." He turned to me.

"Q, you and Angela need to get inside the boat. Seal it up. Close all the doors, hatches, and windows. And lock them tight. I'm leaving Croc with you. And I'm going to use whatever I've got left in the tank to look around for Speed. Maybe there's something at the scene, or maybe I can find something in X-Ray's records. A place he could be hiding. If I can't find him, and once the intellimobile is secure, I'll have Felix and Uly wait here until Blaze and Roger's limo arrives to take you to the concert. They are going to have questions if you're not there. I'll be there. Croc will be there. If Speed tries anything, we'll be ready. Any questions?"

Both Angela and I shook our heads.

Boone disappeared before our eyes.

Back in Charge

Speed had figured out much of it already, but now he knew everything. Because he'd had the boat bugged for a long time. That way he could keep tabs on Q whenever he wanted. As usual, he'd been right: when he returned from the bank with the case, his monitor was blinking with an alert that there were new recordings at that location. It could be the new owners, but he checked just to be sure. It was Boone and Q and his new stepsister. He listened as Boone recounted his story. Q was a sentimental kid and there was a chance he would want to visit his old home.

Speed Paulsen sat in his penthouse apartment staring at the case containing the Holy Grail. He thought back to when he was a young boy moving among the Saracen camps outside Jerusalem. He had heard the rumors. The Knights Templar, it was said, had found something of great power. Some had said it was the Holy Grail or the Ark of the Covenant or the One True Cross. In that primitive time, there were those who believed the Templars were nearly invincible.

The rumors had been true. They had found something powerful.

All Speed had known for certain was that the object he had taken from the injured Templar that night had given him a great ability. The glowing blue light had changed him forever. And to think it was the Holy Grail. The cup of Christ, the prophet. Now, for the first time since he'd wrenched it away from the wounded Boone, he felt like he was finally ready to take its power for his own. For centuries he had tried each and every possible way imaginable to open the box. Not knowing exactly what was inside, he could not risk smashing or cutting it open for fear of destroying what lay within.

For centuries Boone had been looking for the Grail and Speed had been looking for Boone. He had watched from the shadows as Boone had fought off his attackers, using just enough of the power to win. Then he had opened the box and the strange light emanating from it had begun to heal the wounded knight and his dog. Moving quickly, Speed had darted out of the darkness and stolen it from the knight before he could fully recover. Once Speed realized the light he'd been exposed to had given him extended life, he had always assumed that the knight was out there, too, looking for him.

Opening the box now would give him unlimited power. He would destroy the West. All of the infidels would bow before him, or they would die.

Speed stopped to think about the ironic poetry of what was about to unfold in the next few hours, when he forced Boone to open the container. In a way, he admired Boone. The old knight had not forsaken his duty. For nine hundred years he had not given up the search. Though he was doomed to fail, Speed respected his warrior spirit. Many would have given up. But not Boone.

All these years. The magnitude of what they had both accomplished washed over him. Boone had proven a worthy adversary. Now their long mutual pursuit was near its end. It had been epic. But it was time for the old man to die. It would only be right for Speed to be the one to end his life.

Speed picked up the case and set it on the desk. He snapped open the latches and lifted the container from inside. Holding it in his hands, he could swear the power it held inside flowed through him. Now, at last, he would have it completely.

How many hours of his life had he spent trying to find the way to open it? A conservative estimate would be thousands. The Grail was inside a container made of extremely dense hardwood, but it was apparently lined with lead. It had been X-rayed, CAT-scanned, and examined with every imaging device and he still could not see what was inside it. As for the combination, he had run it through every computer simulation and decryption program available, and still he could not open it. But now he knew why. And more important, he knew who could open it for him. Now it had become so simple.

Boone thought he was so smart. Boone believed he could hide. Just like Buddy T., who had learned the hard way there was no escaping Speed Paulsen. Boone now stood at the edge of defeat.

"It's over, Templar," Speed said to the empty room. "Well played. You fought bravely. But the game is done." Then he laughed again.

As soon as Speed had discovered Boone's true identity—and that he was working to find and destroy the ghost cell—Speed Paulsen had been three moves ahead of him.

The takedown at the bank was too easy. He had to give the Leopard credit. She had sensed something was wrong. Too bad she had been unable to do anything about it. He had almost killed her, but he changed his mind; he couldn't resist letting her live. Letting all of them live. That was better. Boone would have no choice but to tell them what had happened and who had hurt them. Now they would wonder for the rest of their lives when he would be coming back to finish the job. Maybe even after he had brought the West to its knees he would let them live. It might be more fun to have Boone and his team and the Leopard always looking over their shoulders for the rest of their lives. Slowly driving them insane might be a great deal more enjoyable than killing them.

Speed sat back on the couch and picked up one of his guitars. It would not be smart to rush his next move. Boone had a thousand years of experience. He was a tracker, a spy, a warrior, and a knight. Though Speed had managed to evade him thus far, he would not be easily duped.

He put down the guitar and picked up a tablet lying on the couch next to him. He touched an icon, and the screen split into two screens. One showed Boone, Q, and that girl sitting on the deck of the boat. On the other screen, he reset the recording to the part where Boone was telling them about his fellow knight building the container that housed the Grail.

Rising to his feet, he paced back and forth in the apartment. What could Boone have planned for him? The last two weeks

or so, Speed had Boone playing defense. Reacting to the
events Speed had set in motion. Would he switch up now?
Would Boone go on the offensive?

As he stalked back toward the couch, a movement on the
tablet caught his eye. Boone had stood up and was issuing
orders to Q and Angela. He must have just learned about the
attack at the bank. Then he disappeared from the screen and
Speed watched as the two kids hustled inside the boat's cabin.
No doubt Boone had ordered them into lockdown.

Now he knew what to do. Boone couldn't keep them there
forever. A plan started to form in his mind.

He sat down on the couch and picked up the guitar. Speed
Paulsen had some thinking to do.

Lockdown

The hospital emergency room was a tidal wave of confusion. Pat Callaghan charged in, dodging paramedics, doctors, nurses, and patients as he tried to make his way to the main counter through the sea of people. There were cops in abundance. The attack at the bank appeared to have sent half of the SFPD to the scene first. Now they seemed to all be at the hospital. Callaghan pulled his Secret Service credentials from his pocket. Holding them over his head, he shouted above the noise.

"Special Agent Pat Callaghan, U.S. Secret Service. Who's in charge here?"

A grizzled, world weary-looking patrol sergeant, his buzz-cut hair tinged with gray, approached him. The nametag above his badge read RHADIGAN.

"At the moment, I am. Sergeant Rhadigan, SFPD," he said. The two men shook hands.

Callaghan handed his credentials to the sergeant.

"I know the drill, so call in and verify my credentials.

In the meantime, get in touch with Captain Larry Quinn on your antiterrorism task force unit. We worked together when I was on presidential detail a few years ago. He knows me. This case—the five wounded vics who were brought here—are agents of the federal government. This is a matter of national security and under the auspices of the Patriot Act, I am taking charge of them, this scene, and the investigation."

Sergeant Rhadigan handed the credentials to a patrolman and instructed him to call them in for verification.

"I know Quinn," he said, frowning. "Give me a minute." The sergeant stepped away. Like most cops he didn't like having to give over jurisdiction to a Fed, but he grabbed the microphone clipped to the shoulder of his uniform and spoke into it for a few minutes. The patrolman returned with the badge case and the sergeant handed it over to Callaghan.

"All right," he said. "You are who you say you are, and Captain Quinn vouches for you too. Says to tell you he's met a lot worse Feds than you. What do you need?"

"I need to talk to the doctor in charge. Then I need all the victims from the attack moved to a secure area. Someplace we can lock down. And I mean lock down completely. No egress by doors or windows."

"That could a problem," Rhadigan said. "From what I understand, four of the vics are currently stable but have some serious injuries. And one is in surgery."

Callaghan silently cursed. He guessed it was Vanessa in the OR. From the security video it looked like she'd suffered the worst wound. How could he secure everyone the way Boone wanted with Vanessa still in surgery? He thought for a moment.

"All right, I've got it. Most hospital ORs have a prep and scrub room for the docs and nurses outside the actual operating room. We're going to move the four other vics there, and then shut everything up tight. Can you get me somebody in hospital administration or the head of the ER? We need to move these people now."

Sergeant Rhadigan disappeared into the crowd and returned moments later with a harried-looking physician. Callaghan told the doctor what he required.

"Impossible. We can't take proper care of patients in that setting, we'd need—"

Callaghan held up his hand.

"What's your name, doctor?"

"Douglas, and I need—"

"Doctor, this isn't a request. It's going to be done now. I don't care what you have to do, but you're going to do it. This is a federal case under the Patriot Act."

The doctor threw up his hands and started shouting orders. The first team member Pat saw was Malak, who was being wheeled out on a stretcher. Her chest and arms were covered in blood, but she was trying to get off the gurney.

"Malak!" he cried and rushed to her side.

"Pat! You've got to get me out of here! Angela! I need to get to Angela!" Again she tried to lift herself off the gurney. He gently pushed her back down by the shoulders.

"Malak! Listen to me," he said. Her eyes were wild and unfocused. "Malak! Angela is fine. She's safe. We've got to get you patched up."

"No, I've got to go to my daughter," she said. "She's in danger."

"Get her up to the OR," Pat told the orderlies. The stream of Malak's loud and angry curses nearly drowned out the noise and confusion of the emergency room as they took her away.

X-Ray came next. He was walking but attached to an IV, with orderlies on either side of him. His hand was wrapped in a massive mound of gauze. Then came Ziv and Eben, on stretchers. For a moment, Pat was struck by how the two of them had been thrown together on this job. They were former enemies, and now they'd almost died together, trying to complete their mission.

Callaghan rode with the SOS team up the elevator to the OR floor. When he stepped off, he followed them through a set of double doors that led to the pre-op area. A surgeon in a blue gown ripped his mask off and stormed up to Callaghan.

"Who are you and what is the meaning of this! You can't bring these people here! We're dealing with seriously injured patients. This is an operating wing. We can't properly take—"

"What is your name, doctor?" Callaghan asked, interrupting and using his "don't mess with me" voice.

"Dr. Simpkins. Robert Simpkins."

"Dr. Simpkins. Is this a hospital or not?"

"What? Yes, of course, but I don't—"

"I thought so. Then you have everything I need. This is a matter of national security. You get whatever equipment, doctors, nurses—anything required to take care of my team up here in the next five minutes. Then this wing is going to be sealed off, and no one is leaving until I say so. Are we clear?"

"You don't have that authority. Not even under the Patriot Act. It clearly states that emergency medical decisions are not subject to—"

Callaghan sighed. He pulled out his phone and pushed a button.

"Boss?" he said into the phone. "Yes. I know you're busy. Sorry to interrupt. I'm here at the hospital. Boone wants everyone moved into an OR wing and to have it sealed off. I'm on it, but there's a problem. I've got a Dr. Simpkins here who doesn't approve. Yes. Yes, sir." Callaghan pushed the speaker button and held the phone in his hand.

"Am I speaking to Dr. Robert Simpkins?" the voice on the phone said.

"Yes . . . who is this . . . what is the meaning—"

"This is President J. R. Culpepper. Do you recognize my voice?"

"I don't believe you . . . and furthermore, this agent Callaghan is disrupting treatment and endangering the health of my—"

"Dr. Robert L. Simpkins," J.R. went on, talking over the sputtering doctor.

"Graduated from UCLA's medical school. Oh. I see you had to take organic chemistry twice as an undergrad. I hear that's where they separate the wheat from the chaff. I thought about being a doctor back in college, but decided on political science instead. You live in a high-end condo at 14845 Pierce in the Marina District. And—"

"Who is this? I demand to know who I'm talking to!" Dr. Simpkins's face was turning red. Callaghan touched a button on the phone and the screen blipped. President J. R. Culpepper's face appeared on the screen.

"Can you hear me *now*, doctor?" he asked.

"I . . . yes, I can . . . Mr. President, and I apologize, but medical protocol states . . . that . . ."

In the corner of the room, a fax machine rang. The machine kicked on and began printing.

"Coming over your fax machine right now is a copy of Executive Order 8354-A. It essentially gives Special Agent Patrick Callaghan of the United States Secret Service authority to do *anything* he deems necessary and requires all personnel at your hospital to obey his orders to the letter. In addition, it also gives him present and future immunity from any criminal or civil liability should he, in his professional judgment, be required to use any means required, up to and including deadly force, in order to ensure the safety of all parties. Is there a window in the room, doctor? Where you can see outside the hospital right now?"

"Ah . . . yes," Dr. Simpkins stammered.

"Go to it. Look outside," J.R. said.

The dazed doctor shuffled slowly to the window. Looking out, he saw a caravan of military vehicles full of U.S. Marines braking to a stop in front of the hospital. They exited the Humvees and personnel carriers and took up positions around the building. Helicopters hovered in the air nearby.

"Doctor." J.R.'s voice came over the speaker. "Come back to the phone."

The doctor walked back to Callaghan, a look of pure astonishment on his face. He peered into the phone.

"Do you understand now? You're not in charge anymore. Agent Callaghan is. He is now officially the boss of you until he decides this incident is over or I send someone to relieve him. You will do what he says, when he says it, without question. Am I clear?"

"Yes, sir," Dr. Simpkins whispered.

"Good. Don't bother me again." J.R. disconnected the call.

"Are we good?" Callaghan said.

"Yes. Of course," the doctor answered. He turned away and immediately began issuing orders to the nurses and orderlies.

From a corner of the ward, a loud scream and the crash of metal hitting the floor echoed in the enclosed space. Callaghan whirled around, instinctively reaching for his weapon. Malak had knocked down an orderly and was limping toward the door, blood trailing across the floor behind her. Somehow she had found the strength to lift herself off the hospital bed.

"Malak," Callaghan whispered, rushing to intercept her. "Malak, you've got to stay here."

"NO!" she cried. "I'm going to Angela. Don't try and stop me, Pat."

"Malak. Quiet," he said, speaking quietly, hoping no one could hear him over the din of the OR. "We need to try to save your cover if we can. You're hurt. You need medical attention."

"Out of the way, Agent Callaghan. Step away from my daughter or you will regret it. We go to Angela. Now." Callaghan looked to his left to see Ziv limping along behind his daughter. His face was as white as mashed potatoes and he looked like he might pass out at any moment. "We don't want to hurt you. But we will if you try to keep us from her."

"Listen, both of you. Angela is safe. Boone has her hidden with Q. Whoever did this can't get to her. Both of you can barely stand. You'll be no good to her until you're patched up."

"I am going–" Malak winced as a needle plunged into her shoulder. The sedative made her instantly woozy and she collapsed forward into Callaghan's arms. Dr. Simpkins stood behind her, holding an empty syringe. Callaghan gave him a thumbs-up and handed Malak off to an orderly.

"That's what I'm talking about, doctor," he said.

"No!" Ziv shouted. He tried to reach Callaghan but his strength left him and he tumbled to the floor. Orderlies and nurses rushed forward and returned Malak and Ziv to their beds.

"Okay," Callaghan said. "Let's get this place locked down." Then, as everyone moved about like a swarm of bees, following his orders, he muttered under his breath, "Boone, I hope you know what you're doing."

MONDAY, SEPTEMBER 15 ⟩

5:30 p.m. to 7:15 p.m. PST

Moving Fast

If I was a nervous wreck before, my mind was racing at about ten thousand miles an hour now. The difference was, I was sitting at the table in the galley of our former sailboat, and Angela was pacing back and forth like a cheetah in a cage. Croc usually slept. But now I could swear he was acting like a guard dog. He would climb the few short steps to the hatch leading to the cabin and smell and examine it, and take a long look though the window. Then he would walk through the galley all the way forward to the sleeping berths. Like he was patrolling the perimeter.

"Angela," I said. "I'm sure if your mom was seriously hurt, they–"

Her beeping phone interrupted me.

"It's Agent Callaghan," she said. "Hello? What happened?" She listened. I could hear his voice over the phone but couldn't make out the words. "Do they . . . she did? He did? Is Vanessa going to be okay? Will you tell my mom I love her when she wakes up? Make sure she knows I'm okay? Thank you." She disconnected the call. The color returned to her face and she visibly relaxed.

"Is your mom okay?"

"Yes." Angela ran her hands through her hair. "Whoever attacked them used a knife. Everyone has terrible cuts and some of them are bad, but they're going to be okay. Vanessa is in surgery, but the doctors think she's going to make it. Agent Callaghan moved everyone up to a surgical ward, and it's locked down tight. Buddy is . . . Buddy is not. He's gone." She bit her lower lip for a few seconds, then let out a large sigh.

"What?"

"Agent Callaghan said my mom was wounded and bleeding, but she climbed out of bed and tried to leave so she could get to me. So did Ziv. They had to be sedated. They're both fine now . . ." She stopped speaking, and her eyes welled up with tears.

"Are you okay?"

"Yes. I just . . . you know . . . It's that you go so long, living your life, trying to do normal things and thinking a certain way. Like how I thought my mom was dead. Then I found out she was alive and what she did and *why* she did it. And it makes me proud. I suppose others might be angry, having been deserted and alone all those years. I mean I had my dad and all, but still . . . I don't know. I'm just so happy she's alive. I don't care about the rest of it. And I have a grandfather. Life is so funny."

"At least your mom is not a supervillain," I muttered.

"Oh, gosh, Q. I'm sorry. I didn't mean . . ." She frowned, and her cheeks reddened with embarrassment.

"It's okay, Angela. Really it is. I'm happy for you. I just . . . It's been my mom and me for so long that Speed is more of a stranger than a father. I mean he's got to be like the world's greatest actor to pull all of this off. No one could actually be as dumb and messed up as my dad pretended to be all those years, without being a real sociopath. For years he made both Mom and me think he was barely able to function as a human being. Now I find out he's a criminal mastermind. I still can't wrap my head around it."

"You need to give yourself a break. You aren't the only one he fooled, Q," she said.

"Well, give the man an Oscar." I was quiet a moment.

"What?" Angela finally prodded me.

"Nothing."

"Yes. Something. You have a tell."

"I do *not* have a tell," I said.

"Yes, you do. When you're curious or have a question about something, you arch your eyebrows."

"I do not," I insisted, immediately de-arching my eyebrows. It's not good for magicians to have tells.

"Well, you've got something on your mind, so spill."

"Do you believe Boone?"

There, I'd said it. I looked away from Angela and around the galley where we were sitting. The Hackworths hadn't changed much. The tabletop was new. The old one had been made of wood and had a chocolate milk stain on it from when I'd spilled a glass once. It had left a dark spot on the wood. There was a window over the sink and they'd hung curtains with little anchors printed on them.

That was about the only change. The granite countertop y the stove was still there. The wood paneling lining the bin walls still felt warm and homey. I missed this boat.

Croc was at the hatch, looking out through the glass ɔ the coming twilight. He swiveled his head around and looked at me and made a curious sound. It was almost as if he understood what I'd said. And that I was questioning my loyalty to his master.

Angela was quiet, like she was giving my question serious thought. "I think I do. Boone believes it. Yes, I believe him. I know I was suspicious and a skeptic at first. But I believe him."

"The Holy Grail," I said. "The Holy Grail. I always thought it was just a story."

"Well, just because—" Angela started to say.

Croc barked, interrupting her.

"Okay," she laughed. "It is the real Holy Grail. But there are all kinds of things in the world that we don't understand and can't explain. Maybe this is just one of those things. Maybe we aren't meant to understand it."

"Like algebra," I said.

She laughed again. She was relaxing. "Not exactly, but there's a saying that what people used to think of as magic hundreds of years ago is now just science. Or something like that. Maybe what Boone found is just an undiscovered element or chemical that gives off properties the way uranium gives off radiation. It just hasn't been discovered or studied. Science and our understanding of the world is changing all the time. Maybe Boone just found this cup that was somehow exposed to or made from some chemical element before anyone else did. Once it's recovered and analyzed we'll know why it does what it apparently does."

It didn't sound so crazy when she explained it like that.

"I guess," I said, getting antsy again. "Before I reach into my pocket and you sigh and roll your eyes, can I get one of my decks of cards?"

"Sure. And while we're waiting, and I know my mom and Ziv are okay, I can do research on it," she said, smiling and pulling her laptop from her backpack. Only Angela could make doing research sound like winning the lottery.

While she tapped away, I shuffled and ran through swivels, flourishes, aerials, and some other one-handed manipulations of the deck. I tried to think about Speed. He couldn't do anything with the Grail without Boone. But still, what would he try next? The ghost cell had always gone to ground after they had staged an attack. At least until recently. They stepped back into the shadows, never taking credit for the things they did. Then they would take weeks, months, sometimes years before doing anything.

Something had changed. Whatever it was, they'd altered their regular methods. They had staged successive attacks in Washington, tried to blow up the USS *Cole* Memorial, kidnapped us in Kitty Hawk, tried to destroy the Alamo Memorial, and launched chemical attacks in several cities. What had triggered the change in behavior? Why weren't Speed and his dirtbag followers disappearing into the shadows like ghosts? He was accelerating. For all these years he'd had the Grail, he just couldn't do anything with it. Now all of a sudden, he takes it out of hiding, kills Buddy, Number Two, at the bank and . . . what? What would he do next?

The bank. He hit Buddy and the SOS crew at the bank. According to Buddy, Speed had given him the Grail with instructions not to tell him where it was. If Buddy had to search his safe-deposit boxes for it, how did Speed know where to hit them? He could have blinked around, watching them. But that would've used up a lot of his energy, according to Boone.

He was watching. Somehow he had eyes on everyone. But could he have enough people to watch all those banks? Or would he use electronic surveillance the way X-Ray did? Could he hack the traffic cams? If he knew Buddy was with Malak and the others, why hadn't he sent another team to take him back?

Why? Then it hit me.

The itch.

Speed had figured it all out. If he had taken down Buddy and Malak and the others outside the bank, it meant he must have figured out Boone was the Last Templar. Somehow he knew Boone was the key. He didn't need to send a team for Buddy. He could wait, watch, and then do just what he had done. Blink in when they found it and take the Grail. But how had he figured it out?

Boone had told no one but Angela and me about the Grail and the container and how it could be opened. If we were the only ones that knew . . .

He was listening.

He'd been listening in the whole time.

I looked around the cabin. Then at the new tabletop.

The new tabletop.

I picked up my cards and started shuffling. I was really letting them fly around. Then I intentionally flubbed a one-handed cut and dropped a bunch of cards on my lap and the floor.

"Dang it," I said. Angela paid no attention.

I bent down underneath the table to retrieve the cards; I looked everywhere on the bottom side of the table. At first I didn't see anything. Then I spotted it. A small flat disk that looked like a battery for a remote control or a hearing aid. It was painted black, just like the post it was stuck to. There was nothing else like it on the post, so I was pretty sure it wasn't part of the table. It was a bug. I was sure of it. What else could it be? And if there was one here in the galley, you could be sure Speed had them hidden all over the boat. And they must have been very high-tech because Felix and Uly would have swept the boat before we got here.

I gathered up all the cards and put them on the table.

"Well, that's enough of that," I said. "Angela, could I borrow your computer one sec? I need to look up something."

"Sure." She turned it around, so it was facing me. I tapped away at the keyboard.

"Ah, there it is. I just thought of some notes for our homework. Maybe the Grail can keep us from going to boarding school," I said.

I took a notebook and pen out of Angela's backpack.

"What's got you so interested in homework all of a sudden?" she asked, confused.

I tried really hard to look and act normal.

"I mean, we're stuck here waiting. We might as well use

the time for something useful, like finding a way to keep us out of boarding school. Boarding. School. In case I haven't mentioned it, I don't want to go. So maybe if we catch up on our homework, maybe if we do some extra credit. How do you think this sounds for the title of our next research paper?"

I had written:

Don't say anything. Act normal. Speed has the boat under surveillance. Definitely bugged, and maybe cameras. Say something about the Grail.

She read the message and, as usual, she didn't show anything on her face.

Angela was going to make a great spy someday.

"That might work. It's an interesting idea. But you know there's more than one version of the story. Are you sure we want to do a paper on this one?"

"Well, I don't know for sure. But look at the details." I pointed to the screen. "If you had it, and if the legends are true, it would be awfully hard not to use it, don't you think?"

"I suppose. So how do we help Boone?"

"I don't know. He knows a lot more about this stuff than we do. I guess we have to sit tight until he gets back."

"You're probably right—"

We were interrupted by a loud knock on the hatch that caused us both to jump and me to make a very embarrassing high-pitched squeal again. I was not cut out for this.

"It's me! Boone," a voice said. "Open up."

Croc barked, and when my heart stopped hammering in

my chest, I stood up and looked through the hatch window. It was Boone. He looked like he did when we were trying to get into the Hancock building in Chicago. His face was pale and sweaty, and he looked exhausted.

"Come on in," I said, opening the hatch. Boone darted in, but then he slammed the hatch shut and I remembered what he said about not being able to blink through something solid.

He was breathing hard.

"Hey, Boone," I said. "You know Angela, she's been researching this whole Holy Grail thing. She found something interesting. We're trying to come up with a title for a research paper. Of course we'd be leaving out your details. What do you think of this for a title?"

I handed him the notebook. Boone played along, reading what I had written. The only thing that showed on his face was a slight narrowing of his eyes.

"Huh. Well, I never would have thought that. But I'd say you're probably on the right track. But you'll have to finish later. Your parents' limo will be here in a few minutes to take you to the concert at the fairgrounds. I'll ride with you. I've got people following. Can you get ready to go?"

"I'm ready right now," I said, and I was. And I knew when Boone said he had "people following" he meant Uly and Felix and maybe some others we didn't know about.

"Q, you've really got to move on from the cargo pants. You could wear something a little more fashionable," Angela said. At first I thought she was picking a fight, but she bit her lower lip to tip me off that she was playing to the microphones.

"Oh, more fashionable? You mean like a ratty backpack?"

I said.

"There's nothing wrong with my backpack," Angela said.

"There's nothing wrong with my cargos," I said.

It was pretty amazing how good we were getting at fake bickering. I remembered earlier today how Angela had kicked the clown in the chest while I was running the three-card monte con. We were getting better and better at playing all these roles a spy sometimes has to play. Like Boone using his good ol' boy drawl whenever he was around our parents. I was pretty sure I was going to screw it up at some point. All I could do was hope Boone caught Speed before it happened.

Angela shut down her computer and stuffed it in her backpack.

Boone's phone rang.

"We'll be right out," he said as he answered. "The limo is here. Let's go."

We left the galley through the hatch. Once on the deck we climbed down the ladder to the dock. The limo was waiting for us in the parking lot. Knowing that Speed could do the same thing Boone could do, it felt like the car was a million miles away. But we couldn't run or sprint or do anything that might tip off anyone who was watching. We had to act normal.

Croc strolled along in front of us, and Boone walked behind us. With each step we took, another bead of perspiration ran down my forehead into my eyes. About halfway there it suddenly occurred to me that Mom and Roger were in the limo. Now I was really nervous. What if Speed showed up and did something to Mom just for spite?

In the end, I realized there was nothing else we could do.

If he showed up or blinked in or whatever, I just had to hope Boone or Croc could somehow take him out. It was a horrible choice, but right at the moment, it was the only one I had.

We had to keep going. We had to find a way to stop Speed.

Taken

Boone paced backstage. The concert was just starting. Blaze and Roger already had the crowd whipped into a full-on frenzy. After the attack at the bank Boone called J.R. and had him send a team to take Buddy's body to a secure facility. Buddy's identity had not been released. If the news got out and Roger or Blaze heard it, it would be game over. Boone also hadn't told Q and Angela yet, but he was reasonably certain Speed was still going to come after Q. He couldn't say why, because he never saw Speed as much of a father. But he still felt in his gut it was going to happen.

The Marin County Fairgrounds had an open-air arena, so there weren't too many places that could be completely sealed off. Boone hoped to keep Q and Angela on the boat. But once Q figured out it was bugged, they couldn't do that. It would be too difficult to keep up the façade and not let Speed know they were on to him.

Besides, Blaze and Roger always insisted on having their kids with them at the concert. With their being shipped off to boarding school soon, they wanted to spend as much time with Q and Angela as possible. But in reality, there was no place that could be truly protected. If Boone didn't catch Speed soon, they wouldn't be safe anywhere.

Croc stayed right at his side as he circulated backstage. When they were alone or out of the line of sight of the crew or backup musicians they would both test a blink. Boone had made another rash decision when he'd blinked away from Q and Angela earlier in the day. He'd let emotion cloud his judgment. Knowing what Speed had done to his team outside the bank had left him thirsting for revenge. He wasn't fully recharged and he'd run his energy down again. He closed his eyes and concentrated. He disappeared and reappeared about fifteen feet away, glancing around to make sure no one had seen him. If Speed came for either Q or Angela, he was going to have to face him at less than full power.

"Croc, old pal, what about you?" Boone said.

Croc disappeared. A few minutes later he came trotting backstage. He had gone a fair bit farther, probably out to the parking lot. He always did. Something in his metabolism allowed him to regenerate faster.

"Show-off," Boone muttered. Croc huffed.

Once they arrived at the concert, and Blaze and Roger went on stage, Boone had Marie and Art take Angela and Q to separate rooms backstage. Neither place was ideal from a security standpoint. The doors could be locked, but they had windows. They had done their best to seal them up. But Speed would likely find a way in if he was determined to snatch one of them.

Boone was pretending to run the concert with his walkie-talkie. In actuality, he'd turned the show over to one of his top roadies to better focus on protecting Q and Angela. He walked stage left, then down a small corridor. Reaching the small supply room where he'd stashed Art and Q, he knocked on the door.

"Art? It's Boone," he said. "Everything okay?"

"We're good. No sign of anything. Here's a tip, though. Don't ever play gin rummy with Q. He cheats," Art said.

"It's not cheating! I don't cheat. You have tells." Boone could hear Q complain. "Boone, when do I get out of here? I'm going a little nuts."

"Soon, I hope, buddy. Hang tight."

Boone crossed backstage and entered an identical corridor stage right. There was a similar room down the hall where he had Marie guarding Angela. When they reached it, Croc went crazy, scratching at the threshold and barking.

Boone rapped hard on the door.

"Marie! Marie! It's Boone, open up."

Croc was doing his best to dig his way through the door, snarling and growling. Boone tried the door, but it was still locked. He heard a groan come from inside and reared back and kicked the door open. Croc rushed in and went straight to Marie, who was lying on the floor, barely conscious.

"Croc!" Boone said. The dog dashed back out through the door. He would check the parking lot and perimeter of the arena and fairgrounds. Boone gently lifted Marie by her shoulders. Her eyes fluttered open. "I need a medic backstage right, the main corridor. Now!" he shouted into the walkie-talkie.

"Marie, what happened?" he asked.

"I . . . I don't know," she whispered. "We were talking . . . then the window glass shattered. Someone threw a rock through it or . . . something." She touched the back of her head with her hand. It came away sticky with blood.

"What happened after that?" Boone asked.

"I . . . I pushed Angela into the corner and got in front of her. I was reaching for my gun. Then the next thing I knew someone hit me. Hard. I landed on the floor. I heard Angela yell something. Then the door opened and closed. I think I blacked out."

"Did you see anyone?"

"That's the strange thing, Boone. I didn't. I never saw anyone. I messed up, Boone, I lost Angela." Tears welled up in her eyes.

"Shh, Marie. You didn't mess up. I did. It's my fault."

A couple of paramedics wheeling a stretcher rushed up, stopping in front of the room. They both hurried inside and knelt to examine Marie. Boone stood up to get out of their way.

"Marie, they're going to take care of you, okay? You're going to be fine."

He backed out of the room and into the corridor. Croc came trotting up, panting and tired. Boone knew if he had spotted anything at all he would be barking and making a fuss, beckoning Boone to follow him. But he stood there with his head down, trying to catch his breath.

"Right under my nose," Boone muttered. "Dang it. Come

on, pal, we've got to get to Q."

Boone and Croc raced across the backstage to the stage left corridor. In his mind, Boone started to see Speed's plan unfolding. He should have known. He should have put Angela someplace more secure. Speed's plan was suddenly clear to him. If he'd taken Q there was a chance Q could be hurt or injured. Now he had Angela.

"I'll bet you a dollar he wants to trade Angela for the Grail," Boone muttered to Croc.

They reached the door. "Art, it's Boone. Open up!" he shouted.

Boone heard movement inside. The door opened a crack and he could just see Art's face. Art was cautious, opening the door a little wider. Boone noticed his right hand was hidden behind his back, no doubt firmly gripping a pistol. He'd put Q directly behind him.

"What's up?" Art asked.

"Listen. Angela has been snatched, and Marie is injured," Boone said. Art's eyes went wide, then his jaw clenched. He was instantly ready to crack someone in the head.

"Who? Who did it?"

"Art, I can't tell you. There's no time. I promise you I'll personally take care of the person who hurt Marie. I give you my word. Paramedics are looking after Marie right now. Go," he said.

Art didn't waste any time. He sprinted through the door and raced down the hallway to find his partner.

Boone punched a number on his cell phone.

"Uly, it's Boone. Listen. Marie is down. Angela has been

taken hostage. I need you and Felix to come to the back of the stage with the Range Rover. Then the two of you are going to stick to Roger and Blaze like bark on a tree. Copy? Get here as fast as you can." He disconnected the call.

"My dad took her, didn't he?" Q asked.

"Yes," Boone answered.

"Will Angela be okay?"

"Yes."

"How do you know?"

"Because I know what he wants."

"What's that?"

"A trade."

"You lost me," Q said. "What does he want to trade?"

"He's going to trade Angela for me and you," Boone said. "Or at least me."

"What? Why?"

"Because he heard the whole story on the boat today. He'd already figured out I could blink. Now he's sure I'm the one who can open the box and give him the Grail," Boone said.

"Where is he?"

"I don't know. I sure wish I had X-Ray available right about now. But that was part of his plan too. He took out everyone so we'd be alone and blind. He probably had a car in the lot and stashed Angela and took off. He could be anywhere by now."

"What are we going to do, Boone?"

"We're going to find her."

MONDAY, SEPTEMBER 15 >

7:15 p.m. to 10:30 p.m. PST

The Trade

Boone and I sprinted to the Range Rover and pulled out onto the highway, leaving the fairgrounds behind. I sat in the passenger seat while Croc stood on the console between us. We had a couple of hours until the concert ended. If we didn't find Angela by then, we'd have a lot of explaining to do.

We drove a few miles down the road in silence.

"Why are we heading into the city?" I asked.

"I don't know. Seems like the most logical direction. More places to hide," Boone said.

"Boone? You really don't know what you're doing here, do you? You're waiting for him to contact you, right?" I said, trying and failing to keep the worry out of my voice. Angela had been my stepsister for about two weeks. And I wanted her safe.

"That's right. Remember something, Q. You figured out that the boat was bugged. I should have suspected as much. Speed has probably had it bugged for a long time. That's on me. But now he knows that the only way he can get to the Grail is through me. And if he harms Angela, he'll get nothing. We got enough info on the ghost cell from Buddy T.'s safe-deposit boxes to keep a dozen agencies busy for months. Membership rolls, finances, training facilities, deep-cover operatives–J.R. is busy taking it apart right now. If Speed doesn't get the Grail, he's back to square one as far as his terror network goes. But his problem has always been ego. He thinks he's smarter and better than anyone. Right now he's thinking the Grail will give him ultimate power. And it could. If he could get to it. He hasn't focused on the fact that even if he does get the box open, he has no more organization, no more operatives. Whatever happens between Speed and me, he's going to be alone even if he comes through this."

"But if he gets access to the Grail, couldn't he use it to raise an army of terrorist blinkers? I mean that's what you and Sir Hughes did, right? You both used its power to fight in the Crusades. It gave you a huge advantage. You said so yourself. Why couldn't Speed do the same?"

"I'm sure that's exactly what he plans to do. He could even do it in secret. Over time, he could put his agents in powerful positions; it would be an infiltration unlike any seen in history. Remember he already got two people inside the White House and they didn't have the power. Imagine what he could do with operatives in government, business, finance. He could bring everything down. The restoration of the Caliphate would be complete."

We were both quiet a moment while we considered it.

"But remember, we know who he is now," Boone said. "The blinking power is not limitless. Eventually, you have to rest and regenerate. Speed could still get caught. Locked up in a sealed place he could never get out of. I don't think we need to worry about all this. Speed is smarter than I gave him credit for, but he will still find a way to screw it up."

"I guess," I muttered. I wasn't so convinced.

"There's one thing that's bothering me, though," I said after a moment.

"What's that?" Boone asked.

"How did Speed figure it all out? I mean when he showed up during Bethany's kidnapping, he was running an op." I actually said op. I'd been hanging around spies far too long. "But on the coach, when you put the tracker in his boots, he knew right away. Then he followed us to San Antonio and it must have been him freaking out Malak in the safe house, in Chicago. How did he put it all together?"

Boone shook his head.

"I don't know, other than, as I said, he's smarter than we gave him credit for. And I've been around a long time. There have been rumors about me and the SOS team out there in intelligence circles for some time now. You can't keep everything a secret. No matter how hard you try. Every side has spies. We all know things about each other. When he saw us there, and had heard the rumors about me being NOC for the CIA, he probably put two and two together. Maybe he didn't know I was the Last Templar but he knew I was involved in bringing down the ghost cell somehow. After that, he probably kept tabs on us by blinking or having Buddy T. track our activities. I don't know exactly."

I thought about it. It was hard to reconcile the Speed I

knew with this new version. My Speed couldn't tie his shoes on a good day. That's probably why he wore cowboy boots all the time. He fooled everyone. Even my mom.

Boone's phone rang. It was synced with the Bluetooth system on the Range Rover, so he pushed the button on the steering wheel.

"Boone."

"Hello, Boone. Or should I say 'Templar'?"

"Hello, Speed. So you're Number One. Hard to believe."

"Ha. Good one. I'd expect something a little more pithy after almost a thousand years, Boone."

"Thank God your vocabulary has improved, Speed. At least you're no longer ending every sentence with 'man.' "

Speed ignored the taunt.

"You do realize I have the girl. Make me mad and she might have a very bad day."

"Nah. I don't think so. You do anything to Angela, and you'll never get what you want."

"Is that right?" I could hear the sneer in his voice over the phone.

"Yep. In fact, I suspect you're running on empty right about now. Angela is the only card you've got, so let me get the warning out of the way. If you–"

"Enough! You've got ninety minutes. You come and bring Q."

"Where?"

"Alcatraz Island on the back side, behind the prison. It's deserted back there and the park is closed. There's a small clearing above the dock. Don't be late." He disconnected.

"This isn't good," Boone said. "I don't have enough energy yet to blink to Alcatraz. How are we going to get there?"

The car was silent as Boone and I tried to think of a way to reach Angela.

"I've got an idea," I said. "Do you still have the little gizmo X-Ray gave you? The one that jams surveillance cameras and microphones?"

"Yes. Why?"

"We can take the sailboat. If you use the device to knock out all the cameras and microphones on the boat we can be sure he won't know we're coming. I mean, I know he's expecting us, but maybe we can sneak up on him or something. At the very least, he won't be able to listen to us."

"That'll work," Boone said. He gave the Range Rover the gas. Heading for the marina.

The Rock

Angela was sitting on a log in a clearing in the underbrush on Alcatraz Island. She had been here several times on school field trips. Spanish explorers had called it Alcatraces. It was originally a fort and lighthouse that helped ships navigate the San Francisco Bay. In the Civil War it had housed Confederate sympathizers and privateers. In 1933 it became a federal prison, and served in that capacity until it closed thirty years later, in 1963. It was a desolate, inhospitable place. And it had earned its nickname, "The Rock."

Her hands were flex-cuffed behind her. A few feet away, Speed Paulsen paced back and forth. The details of how he'd managed to capture her were still fuzzy to Angela. She remembered being in the room backstage at the fairgrounds. Marie was telling her a funny story about Boone. Then the window shattered. Marie had shoved her into a corner and stood in front of her, reaching for her gun.

That was the last thing she remembered. Judging by the throbbing spot on the back of her head, she guessed Speed knocked her out somehow.

It was dark and shadowy back here. Across the bay, she could see lights from Sausalito and the marina where they'd sat on the boat that afternoon. It seemed like forever ago.

As he paced, Speed muttered unintelligible words and phrases. He had just gotten off the phone with Boone. She hadn't been able to hear all of the conversation. But enough to determine that he was working out a way to trade her in exchange for access to the Holy Grail.

She thought about her mom. What would she do in this situation? Easy. She had given up her life and family in order to root out and destroy the most evil terrorist network the world had ever seen. No way would she let Speed get what he wanted. Not even if it meant her own life.

Q had told her about getting free of a pair of flex-cuffs. Contrary to popular belief, they weren't escape-proof. He'd said the trick was not to move or twist your wrists. You used your shoulder and elbow to manipulate your hand. Otherwise, your wrists would swell up, and you'd never get free. She tried it. It was hard. Your instinct was to try and yank your hand out of the cuffs. After a few minutes she gave up. She was not a magician like Q.

She wondered if she could take Speed out with a tae kwan do kick or something. Maybe if she could get him close enough to her she could sweep his legs. Then give him a good hard stomp on the head. *Try blinking away when you're unconscious, you skinny little worm*, she thought.

"You know Boone isn't going to give you what you want," she said. Maybe she could get him talking. Stir him up and get him to make a mistake.

"Shut up." He didn't even interrupt his pacing.

"Boone is too smart for you. He's got resources you can't even–"

Speed stormed over to where she sat on the log.

"I said shu–"

It was the moment she was waiting for. Angela launched herself from the log, aiming the crown of her head toward the point of his chin. *See how you like a nice head butt, weasel face.* But she never connected. Speed was suddenly gone. Angela lost her balance and sprawled face first on the ground. Someone grabbed her roughly by the arms and jerked her to her feet.

"Nice try," Speed said. "But you might say I'm a lot 'speedier' than you. Sit down and behave." He pushed her back onto the log.

She was seething with frustration, but tried not to show it. *Just you wait.*

Speed resumed his pacing. Angela turned her attention to the case holding the Grail. It sat on the ground a few feet away. There was no doubt in her mind that Boone and Q were on the way. But she needed to try and do something to even up the odds.

"This is epic," he said. "Perfect place to have a showdown with that fool Boone. Did you know that Machine Gun Kelly and Al Capone were prisoners here? They were the baddest of the bad. Until me."

"Really? The baddest of the bad? You? I don't think so. Unless you're talking about how you dress. Then you might have a case," Angela said.

Speed ignored her and looked at his watch again. He pulled his phone out of his pocket and the screen lit up, illuminating his face. He still wore full Speed regalia. His hair was braided with feathers. His ears were pierced about a dozen times with a variety of earrings and posts. On his feet were fancy cowboy boots made, no doubt, from some exotic animal skin. Angela had been around musicians most of her life, so she was used to unusual dress. But she still thought Speed looked ridiculous.

She watched his face closely as he studied the screen. His eyes narrowed and he tapped the phone a couple of times, giving it a small shake, as if something wasn't working. He put it in his pocket and glanced out at the bay.

"Listen," he said to her. "I'm going to go do some looking around. You had better be here when I get back. This is an island, remember. There's nowhere for you to go."

"Duh," Angela said. "You brought me here in a boat, remember? Must be a bummer you never learned how to blink with someone who can't."

"Blink? What are you talking about?"

"Boone has learned how to blink with someone who can't. All he has to do is hold them by the arm or something, and they go along with him. But since you brought me here on a boat, I guess you never figured it out."

"First of all I don't blink, I speed. And he can't do that. You can't speed with someone who doesn't have the ability. I should know, I tried," Speed said. But he didn't sound entirely convinced.

"Don't you get it? You think you're the one who's a step ahead. Boone's been on to you since we arrived in Philadelphia at the start of the tour. Why do you think everything you've tried has blown up in your face? My bet is he's already here. He's probably got a couple of his guys with him staring at you through the sights of a sniper rifle right now. You're six kinds of toast."

Speed glanced around, looking over his shoulder, his eyes darting back and forth.

"You're lying."

"Yeah, but according to Boone you were only exposed to the Grail power for a short time. Boone used it numerous times. You should see some of the stuff he can do. It's pretty amazing. If I were you, I'd just surrender now and save yourself the embarrassment." Q always said she was an exceptional liar. All she could hope was that Speed would buy it.

"Shut up!" Speed stalked back and forth in the clearing. He looked out at the bay. There were boats moving across it, but none of their running lights indicated they were heading in the direction of the island. Of course, they could be running dark.

"Where is that old geezer?" Speed muttered. Then he blinked away.

She was surprised he left the metal case behind. Angela assumed the wooden container Boone had described to them was inside it. She stood up and hustled over to it. Turning around, she squatted down, grabbing the handle with both hands. She stood and lurched away. It was hard to walk and carry the case like this, with her arms bound behind her. But she had to try. Maybe she could hide it, or if she could get to the water–

She yelped as Speed appeared right in front of her.

"Going somewhere?" He reached around her and yanked the case out of her hands. He jerked her back into the clearing, shoving her back onto her seat on the log.

"Nice try. You're a brave kid, Ashley. But there's nobody here. Boone isn't here. We're alone. Now stay put."

"The name is Angela, you moron. And sure. I'll stay put. That way I'll have the best seat in the house to watch Boone take you down."

Speed smirked and stalked off to the edge of the clearing, looking out over the bay. Angela felt a little deflated. Nothing she tried was working.

As her head drooped in dejection, she looked down to find that the angel necklace her mother had given her years ago had fallen outside her shirt during their tussle. The sharp edges of the wings gave her an idea. Bending at the neck, she swung her head back and forth until the chain flew up. She grabbed it in her teeth. Turning to the side, she bit down as hard as she could until she felt the chain snap in two. Slowly she let one end of the chain out of her mouth, and the angel pendant dropped onto the log next to her. She then twisted the other way. With her hands still bound behind her, she felt around until she found the charm with her left hand. Picking it up, she gripped it tight and turned it over in her hand until the wings were facing out.

She smiled as Speed stood with his back to her. With the charm tight against the flex-cuffs, she started using the angel's wing as a saw. It was slow going, and she couldn't see, but after a moment she got a rhythm going and could feel the pendant cutting into the plastic.

Speed was in for a big surprise.

Over the Bounding Seas

In our haste to get off the boat when the limo arrived, I had forgotten to return the sailboat keys to the marina office. They were still in my pocket. This is what you call lucky, because the marina office was locked up tight, and we sure didn't have time to look for another boat.

My mom was a really good sailor. She'd taught me a lot, but not everything. Mainly we just lived on the boat and didn't take it out all that often. Sailing is a lot of work. But it was actually cheaper living on the boat than having a house or apartment in San Francisco. And infinitely cooler.

I started up the engines and backed out of the slip, then steered toward the breakwater. Once we passed it, we'd be in the bay and could set a course for Alcatraz. There was only one problem. The "I wasn't much of a sailor" thing. Like I said, my mom had taught me a lot. But not everything. From looking at the gauge, I wasn't even sure if we had enough fuel to make it all the way to the island using only the engines. We'd have to raise the sails, and that's where I'd run into problems.

Boone had activated X-Ray's gadget that would scramble all the audio and video signals coming from the boat. I knew Speed couldn't track us electronically. But sailing is not easy. In fact, it is hard and takes a lot of knowledge. I could operate the boat with the engines running. But hoisting the sails and navigating was a whole different story.

We were almost to the breakwater when I realized I was going to need some help.

"Um, Boone," I said.

"Yes."

"You've been alive for a long time, right?"

"Yeah."

"I don't suppose you've ever learned to sail in all that time, have you?"

"A little."

"How little?"

Boone pointed to the mast. "That's the mast. That rolled-up canvas attached to it is the sail," he said.

"Seriously? All that time on your hands and you never learned to sail?"

"I never learned to do a lot of things."

I groaned. "I hope we have enough fuel to get there."

"If we don't, we'll figure it out," Boone said.

Off in the distance I could see the lights on Alcatraz.

"So why didn't you ever learn to sail?" I asked.

"Well, I've been alive for over nine hundred years, Q. Give me some credit for learning how to do a lot of other stuff."

"Really? How many languages do you speak?"

"Thirty-one."

"How did you end up in the music business?"

"Don't really know. I always liked music. And after the Second World War, British and American music became enormously popular all over the world. One thing I haven't picked up in my long life is musical ability. So I couldn't be a musician. But working with musicians and bands got me into and out of a lot of countries without questions. American music was welcome in a lot of places Americans weren't."

"How many presidents have you known?"

"A few. Not all. Every few years I had to take a break. I'd 'retire' and move off someplace for twenty or thirty years, until people forgot about me. Then I'd come back with a new name and identity and work my way up the chain. It usually didn't take long. Blinking made it easy for me to get good intelligence, and that gets you noticed by the higher-ups. But it's been a challenge the last thirty or forty years. There are too many cameras and computers. Everything is recorded and stored. Even really old photographs have been scanned and put online now. As you discovered with your pal P.K."

"And you've been looking for the Grail this whole time?" I asked.

"Yep. It was my duty to keep it safe. I lost it," Boone said.

"But you were injured; it wasn't your fault."

"Doesn't matter. Duty is duty. Sure, I suppose I could give up and stop looking. But in truth, I couldn't risk letting something that powerful fall into the hands of someone who might misuse it. And I couldn't take a chance that someday, with all of this technology that keeps getting invented, someone wouldn't figure out a way to open Quintas's container and get access to it."

"Did you ever want to give up?"

Boone laughed. "Plenty of times, Q. There have been hundreds of moments when I thought that maybe whoever took it lost it themselves. Or hid it and died, and it would never be found. At first, all I knew was that it let me blink and healed wounds. I had no idea it would also make me live such a long time. But then . . ."

"But then what?"

"It sounds weird when I say it."

"Really, Boone? It sounds weird? In case you haven't been keeping up on current events, we passed weird about three counties back."

Boone chuckled. "You've got me there. For a while now, I've had this hunch it was keeping me alive until I found it. I know how strange that sounds. And it makes no logical sense. But there's always been this feeling I've had. Like it's out there waiting for me to recover it. Almost like I made a promise the Grail is waiting for me to keep."

I was quiet a few minutes.

"Boone?"

"Yeah?"

"Ever since we found out about Speed, and about him being Number One . . . I can't stop thinking about what happened to me in Chicago. When I blinked."

"Mm-hmm. I know what you're thinking, Q. You don't have to worry about it."

"How do you know what I'm thinking?"

"When you've lived as long as I have, you learn how to read people. You're worried that, since your dad can blink and he's a bad guy, you'll end up using it to do bad things like he does. Am I right?"

He was right. That was exactly what I was worrying about.

"Well . . . yeah. I mean, haven't you ever been tempted to do something . . . I don't know . . ."

"Evil? Listen, Q, temptation is part of being human. Once I was playing poker with Doc Holliday, the famous gunfighter. I blinked behind him to look at his hand. Then I blinked back into my seat before anyone noticed. He was bluffing, and I won. I cheated in a poker game. He was a mean little snake, so I didn't feel too bad about teaching him a lesson. And that's just one example. But you don't have to worry."

"Why? What if I do something I'm not supposed to?"

"You won't."

"How can you be sure?"

"Because you have a conscience, Q. You have morals. Your dad doesn't, but you do. Just because you're the son of a bad guy doesn't automatically make you bad. And we don't even know if you have the same level of ability that Speed and I do. But even if you do, you won't use it except to help people."

"You sound pretty confident."

"I am."

Boone seemed so sure of himself. He looked at his watch.

"We've got about twenty minutes," he said, closing his eyes and appearing to concentrate. "We're close to the island. But I still don't have enough gas in my tank to blink there. Croc?"

I was conflicted. I knew we had to rescue Angela and time was critical. But I was secretly glad Boone wasn't leaving. If he did, I'd have to pilot the boat and would probably run it up on the rocks and die horribly.

Croc sat up on his haunches and huffed.

"Can you do it, buddy? Can you get there? Find Speed?"

Croc was gone in the blink of an eye.

Croc

Croc materialized in the water about one hundred yards off shore. He shook his head and paddled hard. *Long way to the island,* Croc thought. He had been with Boone so long he almost always immediately understood what Boone wanted him to do.

"Find Speed," Boone had said. Croc blinked and now he would do what Boone asked. He only wished he hadn't landed in the water.

Unlike Boone, he did regenerate fairly fast. But even he did not have enough power yet to make it all the way to the island. Croc didn't like water. Not because he couldn't swim; he began paddling toward shore immediately. Croc didn't like getting wet because it ruined his smell. After a dip in the ocean, it would take him days to get back to smelling the way he liked. He huffed and paddled harder.

He was aware that humans found his odor offensive. And he didn't care. They had no idea what it was like to be a dog. Humans relied on eyesight and hearing, but to a canine the sense of smell was king. Dogs had better hearing than humans too. Could hear things in higher and lower frequencies than the human ear. But their ability to sniff out different scents and odors, compared to humans' abilities, was like comparing an elephant to an ant.

Croc had been with Boone since he was a pup. They had traveled together all over the world. And he could remember every single thing his nose had smelled in all that time. That was why, when the other human, the one Boone called Speed, was on the coach, Croc had gone so crazy. It was him. The one. He had taken what Boone was searching for all these years.

But despite his special abilities, Croc could not always communicate. Boone hadn't understood. The human had changed, aged. He had been a boy when he took away the glowing thing Boone carried. But his scent had stayed the same. And Croc remembered it. He remembered tracking him in the desert when the boy had taken the glowing thing, until he lost the scent. In the warehouse, when he found the feather, the odor of the one was everywhere. Q had understood.

And now, with the wind coming off the island and over the water, he could again smell the human Boone sought. He was there somewhere. Croc kicked his legs and strained and pushed and finally reached the shore. He was tired and shook his body, water spraying everywhere. He put his nose in the air. The breeze carried thousands of odors. He sorted through them until he found the two he wanted: the human who had taken what Boone wanted, and the girl. Boone called her Angela. Croc liked Angela. Her smell was close by the man

Boone wanted. Her scent also told him she was scared. He would help Boone find the man and save Angela.

He shook the water from his coat one more time and crept away into the darkness.

Showdown

"Here they come," Speed said.

Angela looked up. She could see, a few hundred yards off shore, the sailboat approaching the dock. Boone and Q were coming. She was relieved but still nervous.

"Well, I guess this is it for you, then," she said.

"You know, you got a mouth on you. Somebody ought to do something about that," Speed said.

"You honestly think you can take down Boone?" Angela couldn't help herself: she snorted.

"That old roadie? You think he's special? He's nothing. You're nothing. Your father is a no-talent hack and he married a—well, I was married to Blaze. I wish him luck." Speed was gloating.

"A no-talent hack? Their first album has already gone double platinum, you idiot. Ever had a *double* platinum album, Speed? Ever had a platinum-of-any-kind album? That replica Grammy belt buckle you wear all the time? You won it for 'Best Engineered Album.' That's a production category.

Essentially it means other, more talented people made you sound good. My dad has won four Grammys for 'Song of the Year.' Blaze has won more Grammys and American Music Awards than I can count. Just because you can play the guitar fast, Speed, doesn't mean you can play it well. You've had nine hundred years to practice and my dad is still a better guitarist than you." Angela, despite her circumstances, was enjoying antagonizing Speed. She felt bad for Q for having to put up with this loser all those years.

Without warning, Speed was right in her face. It startled her. How was it possible for someone to move so quickly? She still couldn't wrap her mind around it.

"He is not! Nobody plays guitar better than me! *Nobody!* You got that?"

"Oh. I'm sorry. Does the truth hurt? You made a lot of money in the music business. But it was all because of a well-packaged image. And probably because Buddy T. knew everyone in the industry, and you used proceeds from all the stuff you've stolen over the years to buy your way onto the charts. I mean nine hundred years, and all–"

Her words were cut off when Speed grabbed her roughly by the chin and squeezed.

"Listen," he hissed. "You better shut your mouth. You're lucky I need you to get the Grail. One more word and I . . ." He gave her a little shove and stalked off.

The entire time Angela was talking she was sawing away at the flex-cuffs with her angel charm. Her fingers were cramped, and her wrists were rubbed raw by the plastic. But she refused to quit.

Finally, she felt the cuff give way. She was loose! While Speed had his back turned, she slipped the angel pendant in her pocket so she wouldn't lose it. Then she put her hands behind her back again. She wanted to maintain an element of surprise.

She heard something moving in the underbrush behind her. The moonlight was just bright enough for her to see his outline. Croc! Croc was here.

Then he disappeared.

Turnabout

The fuel guage was almost on empty, and I was relieved we had enough to make it. The hull touched the bumper on the dock. I hopped off and secured the lines fore and aft. Boone stepped off and waited until I was finished.

"I'm up here, Boone!" Speed's voice came out of the darkness. "I can see you. I've got the girl. Don't try anything tricky. I'm holding the Grail. If you make one wrong move, I'm gone."

Boone didn't answer.

"What's your plan?" I asked.

"Don't have one. Going to walk up there and see how it plays out."

"That's it? That's your plan? You've had nine hundred years to think about this and that's all you've got?"

Boone was not really paying attention to me. Maybe he was trying to come up with an improved strategy. Jeez. Seems like he would have given this just a little more thought before now. Maybe jot something down on the back of an envelope?

I mean, couldn't he have had X-Ray invent some kind of force-field ray gun or something? Anything would be better than the "I'm going to walk up there and see how it plays out" plan.

"Let's go. Stay behind me." He started up the dock toward the small rise. I was more than happy to stay behind him. Boone walked along like he was on his way to the store to pick up a gallon of milk. Maybe when you've been at the Alamo and probably punched Hitler in the face and stuff, Speed Paulsen is not so scary, even if he can move faster than the eye can see. I, as usual, felt like I could crawl right out of my skin. It was the first time I could ever remember being so nervous that I didn't even think shuffling a deck of cards would help.

We climbed up the little hill, then walked a few more yards through the underbrush. Then the weeds and bushes diminished and we found ourselves in a clearing. Speed was standing there with one hand on the case, and he had Angela in front of him with a really big knife at her throat. It was getting darker by the minute.

"Far enough, Boone. Don't make any sudden moves or she gets it. This is the same knife I used on all your pals at the bank. It's real sharp. One of my favorites."

Boone didn't say anything, just stared hard at Speed.

"Is that you, Q?" Speed said. "Come on out where I can see you. Slowly."

I stepped out from behind Boone.

"It's cool you came along. Once Boone gives me what I want, I'm going away from here. I want you to come with me. Listening to you on the boat today, I heard you talk about what happened in Chicago. Apparently you can do what Boone and I can do. So I figured we could go off together. I could teach you a few things about this whole deal."

I wanted to vomit. It took me a moment to compose myself.

"Understand something, *Speed*. I'm not going anywhere with you. Ever. Not if you were the last person on earth."

As usual, when it came to me, Speed didn't react at all. He just shrugged.

"That's cool. Whatever. It's your choice. I just wanted to ask you face-to-face. It's a mistake. But it's yours to make," he said.

I'm not somebody who gets angry easily, but right then I was madder than I'd ever been. I wasn't a son to him. I was an experiment, a bauble, a little trinket he could trot out whenever he felt like it, like one of his stupid feathers.

"All right, Boone, tell me how to open the container or you're going to have a lot of explaining to do about how you got her killed."

Boone shook his head. "It doesn't work that way, Speed."

"What?" He pulled Angela closer with his arm and pressed the knife against her neck. She tried not to show anything, but I could tell she was scared. I didn't blame her. Speed was nuts.

"I told you not to try any tricks, Boone," Speed said. "You must want her to die."

"I don't want her to die. I'm trying to explain to you, I can't *tell* you how to open it. *I* have to open it. The box was designed so only I could access it. The grooves in the side were carved to fit my hands alone. The combination only works if

I'm holding it and applying the right amount of pressure at the right time. That's why you've never been able to open it, genius."

"I don't believe you," Speed said.

Boone shrugged. "Well then, I hope you brought a book because we're going to be here all night."

Speed looked angry and confused. He wasn't like I'd seen him before. He was intense. Maybe too intense. He wanted the Grail so bad he couldn't think straight. Which made him even more dangerous.

"I guess exposure to the Grail makes you fast, not smart," Boone said. "Then I suppose we're at an impasse, Speed. The only way you're going to get the Holy Grail is if you hand it over to me."

The Big Finish

I couldn't believe Boone was actually considering this. Neither could Angela.

"Don't do it, Boone," she said. "Don't open it–"

Her words were choked off as Speed jerked her tighter around the neck. The knife was digging into her skin.

"Angela!" I started toward her but Boone put his hand on my shoulder to stop me.

"This is the only way, Speed. You've had it for nine hundred years. Have you ever gotten close to opening it? Why would I lie with Angela's life on the line?"

"Because you're a liar?" Speed responded. But something was happening to him. He was getting all nervous and jerky. I knew this look well. It always happened whenever he didn't get his way. He was about to throw a tantrum.

"Speed. Give me the case. Let me open the box and you let the girl go. Then we all go our separate ways."

There was a storm brewing in Speed; I could see it in his face. But in the end he couldn't walk away. His greed and thirst for power won out.

"All right," he said. He set the case down and backed slowly away with Angela. "You do your thing. But you make one wrong move, and you know I'll kill her. And not even you will be able to move fast enough to stop me."

Boone slowly walked toward the case. He bent down and flipped open the latches and removed a wooden cylinder. He stood and went to work. I remembered he said there were sixteen numbers in the combination. The numbers were carved into a series of wooden rings that encircled the cylinder. As Boone twisted each one into place, it clicked. It was so quiet and tense each click sounded as loud as a gunshot.

Boone then placed his hands around and over the ends. It was exactly as he'd described it: his fingers fit perfectly into the grooves. He twisted the cylinder back and forth in a series of specific movements. There was a loud snapping sound.

It was open. Boone pulled the ends of the cylinder apart. At first nothing happened. Then a weird blue light began glowing inside the cylinder. It was dim at first, but then it got brighter and brighter, lighting up the clearing like a lantern.

Boone turned the cylinder so that the light washed over me and Angela.

"Hey!" Speed shouted. Angela elbowed him in the ribs and Speed involuntarily lowered the knife from her throat.

"Ow!" he yelled.

Boone snapped the container shut and the light disappeared. Dropping it to the ground he leaped forward and kicked the knife out of Speed's hands. His hands were a blur as he landed a combination of punches on Speed's face, gut, and body.

Speed was rocked at first, but recovered and punched back. They kicked at each other, then disappeared, reappearing all over the clearing, slugging and gouging each other. They rolled on the ground. Boone was giving as good as he got, but he was weakening.

Finally, he stopped blinking. Speed didn't, though. He appeared in front of Boone and hit him hard in the face, driving him to his knees. Then he was gone, a second later materializing behind Boone and kicking him between the shoulder blades. Boone collapsed face first in the dirt.

Speed looked at me. Reaching behind him he pulled out a gun and pointed it at Boone. He was going to kill him.

I felt a momentary sensation of dizziness. Then everything in my sight seemed to be moving past me. It was as if everything around me had gone into slow motion. I didn't realize yet that I was moving.

There was a resounding crack as Speed pulled the trigger. I could see the first tendrils of smoke emerging from the gun barrel. Faster I went, until I left my feet, leaping through the air. I was focused on the barrel of the gun, but I could see everything happening around me.

Croc materialized out of thin air and his jaws closed over Speed's gun arm. With a sickening crunch, he clamped down as Speed threw back his head and the first sound of the scream of pain escaped his lips.

The bullet had just left the gun barrel and he dropped the gun. It seemed to fall from the air slowly, as if it were a deflating balloon twirling its way toward the ground. Then as

I gained momentum, things seemed to move faster. I was in the air and I watched as the bullet punched its way into my shoulder. Its impact was stunning, twisting me in midair, but not before I saw Angela coming up behind Speed with the metal case in her hand. She swung from her heels and there was a sickening crunch as the box connected with his head.

Croc still had hold of his arm, biting and growling. Speed slumped to the ground like a curtain falling from its rod. He was out.

I was twisting in the air, and started my own string of loud painful wails as the bullet stopped in my shoulder tissue. I remember thinking how shocked I was at the unimaginable pain of a gunshot wound. When I hit the ground, the motion and movement of the world around me returned to normal. And then came wave after wave of unrelenting agony.

"Ow. Ow. I've been shot!" I cried.

Angela didn't waste a second. She dropped to her knees beside me and put pressure on my shoulder wound to stop the bleeding. And also to make it hurt worse.

"AHH! OH! THAT HURTS!" I screamed. As I twisted my head back and forth, I happened to see Croc licking Boone's face. Slowly he stirred, groaning as he rolled over and clambered to his hands and knees. Speed was unconscious and looked as if he'd be out for a while.

"Q!" Boone said, as he cleared his head. He glanced around the clearing, his eyes falling on the wooden container that held the Holy Grail. "Hang on, buddy," he said. With a groan he crawled to it, snatched it up and rose to his feet, staggering back to where I lay in the dirt, bleeding. Croc took the opportunity to lick my face now and I was in too much pain to complain.

Boone's hands worked the wooden rings on the container and then slid over the ends of it. With a push and a click, it popped open and the blue light leaked out of the inside. Boone held it so it washed over me and himself but not Speed.

I couldn't believe what happened next. The bullet simply reversed its path and popped out of my shoulder. The entry wound closed up and the pain went away. I looked up at Boone and the cuts and bruises on his face were healing up as well. In a few seconds he looked like he always had.

We all got to our feet. Croc went over to Speed and stood guard over him. If I didn't know better, I would have said he looked like he kind of wanted him to come to so he could bite him again.

I rubbed my shoulder. My shirt was torn from the bullet hole, but otherwise I was fine.

"Did I just see what I thought I saw?" I said. "The bullet just popped out of my shoulder?"

"What now?" Angela asked.

Boone rolled Speed over on his stomach and pulled a pair of flex-cuffs from his jeans pocket.

"It's over. I'm going to take him someplace where he can't ever get out. He'll never be able to harm anyone again," Boone said. He reached into his pocket for his phone, putting it to his ear.

"J.R.? It's Boone. It's over. I got him." We could hear the hum of J.R.'s voice but not what he was saying.

"Nope. He's mine. I'm taking care of him. You'll never

have to worry again. And J.R.? This is it for me. You won't see me again. I just want to say it's been an honor."

This time we could hear J.R. yelling, "Boone! Boone!" before Boone disconnected the call.

Boone sighed and looked out at the twinkling lights of Sausalito. Then he turned his gaze to us.

"You're coming back, right?" Angela said. Boone smiled at her and shook his head.

"No, I'm not. This is the end of the line for me now. I don't know why. But I have a feeling that once I get the Grail to safety, I'll get to live out the rest of my years and that will be it," he said. "Same with Speed."

"But . . . Boone?" Angela's voice cracked, and her eyes were filling with tears. I had to admit I was feeling the same way.

"It's okay, Angela," he said. "You can be with your mom now. She's safe and so are you. I just want you both to know something important. In nine hundred years the two of you are the best—" He cleared his throat and his voice cracked.

"Boone, you can't leave," Angela said.

Boone looked at both of us, and his eyes misted over. Then he recovered and returned to normal—spy, guy in charge, issuing orders.

"I have to. You'll be okay. Call Callaghan at the hospital and tell him the threat has been neutralized. Then tell him I had to take off. Everyone is used to me coming and going. It won't seem that unusual. Good-bye, Q. Good-bye, Angela. It's been—"

He didn't wait around. Boone, Speed, and Croc blinked

away. They were just gone. The greatest magic trick ever.

"It's been what?" I said quietly.

Neither one of us said anything more for a few minutes. We tried to take it all in, but there were so many questions it was giving me a headache.

"Angela," I said. "I just thought of something."

"What?"

"We're stranded on Alcatraz Island."

"Stranded? Didn't you bring the sailboat?"

"Yes. But . . ."

"But what?"

"I don't really sail all that well."

"What? You lived on it for years!"

"Lived on it. Not sailed it."

"We'll just use the engines," she said matter-of-factly.

"Okay. But we're almost out of gas."

She bit her lower lip. Considering I'd just been shot, I guess she decided against chewing me out.

"All right. Speed had to have brought me here on a boat. If we can find it maybe we can figure out how to work it or something. If not we'll have to call for help. That's going to lead to a lot of questions."

We walked away from the clearing and back toward the dock. Both of us jumped a little when Croc reappeared right in front of us. At least I thought it was Croc. He looked like Croc, but he was younger. Friskier.

"Is that . . . ?" I said.

"What the—" Angela said. "How did . . . ? It's gotta be Croc . . . he just poofed! but, how did . . . ?"

I remembered that back on the coach at Kitty Hawk, when Croc went after Speed, for a brief moment I thought he'd looked younger. It was like he wasn't the same old creaky dog. The gray hairs around his snout had disappeared and his teeth were not old and yucky. He looked, in fact, a lot like the dog sitting on its haunches in front of us right now.

"That can't be," Angela said. Croc whined and then his stomach rumbled. Loudly. We instinctively took two big steps back.

"It's definitely him," I said.

"What's he doing here? He left with Boone," Angela said.

"I don't know. Did Boone forget something?" I wondered. Croc whined and shook his head back and forth.

"There's a piece of paper in his collar," she said. She walked up to him and pulled it loose. It was too dark to read, so she used the flashlight app on her phone.

"It's from Boone," she said.

Dear Angela and Q,

Croc and I said our good-byes. I sent him back to help you out and keep an eye on you. Remember I told you how the power affects him differently? Well now you can see. You can tell your parents I had to leave for personal reasons and I got you your own "Croc" from my breeder as a gift. Don't worry about the sailboat. Uly and Felix will take care of it. Everything will work out. All both of you need to do is give Croc a belly rub.

Take care,

Boone

"A belly rub?" I said. "What do you suppose that means? Is it some kind of code? In case no one noticed, I just got shot. Actually shot! And it hurt! Then the bullet popped out of my shoulder and it was all covered in blood and goo! That's totally worse than pigeon poop! Way worse! I have had it with all this spy stuff!"

Angela pointed to Croc, who was now on his back with his paws in the air. "I don't think it's code. I think it means give Croc a belly rub."

We bent down, and when we put our hands on Croc's belly there was a blinding flash of light. When the light passed, I looked around and found we were back at the Marin County Fairgrounds.

"What just happened?" I felt a little dizzy again, but not as bad as the time in Chicago.

"I think we just blinked," Angela said. "Whoa." She stood up and staggered a little, feeling dizzy herself.

Croc barked.

"I guess that confirms it," Angela said.

Croc trotted along in front of us as we headed toward the arena.

"Angela?"

"Yeah?"

"You know how you recorded Boone's story? Do you think it's a good idea for us to have that? What if someone found it, or it got out somehow?"

Angela pulled the digital recorder out of her pocket and pressed delete. Then she dropped it on the ground and crushed it with her foot for good measure.

"Now we don't ever have to worry about anyone accidentally learning the truth about Boone," she said. Croc looked back at us and barked and we strolled toward the rear of the stage.

The crowd was shouting "Encore! Encore!" and we heard the music start. The perfect harmony of Mom's and Roger's voices sent the crowd into a thunderous ovation. They truly were a Match.

The three of us walked along silently as the opening notes of "Rekindled" echoed through the autumn night.

The End

Roland Smith

Roland Smith is a *New York Times* best-selling author of twenty novels for young readers and more than a dozen nonfiction titles and picture books. Raised in the music business, Smith has incorporated his experience into the I,Q series. When he's not at home writing, Smith spends a good part of the year speaking with students at schools around the country. Learn more about the I,Q books at www.iqtheseries.com. Learn more about Roland Smith at www.rolandsmith.com.

Michael P. Spradlin

New York Times best-selling author Michael P. Spradlin has written more than twenty books for children and adults. He is the author of The Killer Species series and the international best-selling The Youngest Templar trilogy. He lives in Michigan and can be visited on the Web at michaelspradlin.com.